Hunter's Rain

A J

Dirk Patton

Dirk Patton
Text Copyright © 2016 by Dirk Patton

Copyright © 2016 by Dirk Patton

All Rights Reserved

This book, or any portion thereof, may not be reproduced or used in any manner whatsoever without the express written permission of the copyright holder or publisher, except for the use of brief quotations in a critical book review.

Published by Reaper Ranch Press LLC

PO Box 856

Gilmer, TX 75644-0856

Printed in the United States of America

First Printing, 2016

ISBN-13: 978-1539478447

ISBN-10: 1539478440

This is a work of fiction. Names, characters, businesses, brands, places, events and incidents are either the products of the author's imagination or used in a fictitious manner. Any resemblance to actual persons, living or dead, or actual events is purely coincidental.

Hunter's Rain
Table of Contents

Also by Dirk Patton 5

Author's Note 7

1 10

2 20

3 31

4 36

5 44

6 51

7 60

8 67

9 76

10 86

11 92

12 101

13 109

14 116

15 126

16 134

17 145

18	151
19	157
20	167
21	177
22	189
23	196
24	202
Epilogue	210

Hunter's Rain
Also by Dirk Patton

The V Plague Series

Unleashed: V Plague Book 1

Crucifixion: V Plague Book 2

Rolling Thunder: V Plague Book 3

Red Hammer: V Plague Book 4

Transmission: V Plague Book 5

Rules Of Engagement: A John Chase Short Story

Days Of Perdition: V Plague Book 6

Indestructible: V Plague Book 7

Recovery: V Plague Book 8

Precipice: V Plague Book 9

Anvil: V Plague Book 10

Merciless: V Plague Book 11

Fulcrum: V Plague Book 12

Hunter's Rain: A John Chase Novella

Exodus: V Plague Book 13

Dirk Patton

Scourge: V Plague Book 14

Fractured: V Plague Book 15

Brimstone: V Plague Book 16

Abaddon: V Plague Book 17

Cataclysm: V Plague Book 18

Legion: V Plague Book 19

The 36 Series

36: A Novel

The Void: A 36 Novel

Other Titles

The Awakening

Fool's Gold

Author's Note

Genocide: the deliberate and systematic killing, in whole or in part, of an ethnic, racial, religious or national group.

For decades, the Democratic Republic of Congo has been embroiled in violence that has killed as many as 6,000,000 people. An estimated 45,000 more die each month. The death toll is largely due to widespread disease and famine resulting from ongoing war, and reports indicate that almost half of the individuals who have died are children under the age of five. The conflict has been the world's bloodiest since World War II. The First and Second Congo Wars, which sparked the worst of the violence, involved multiple foreign armies and investors from Rwanda, Zimbabwe, Angola, Namibia, Chad, Libya, and Sudan, among others, and has been so devastating that it is sometimes called the "African World War."

Fighting continues in the eastern parts of the country, destroying infrastructure, causing physical and psychological damage to civilians, and creating human rights violations on a mass scale. Rape is used as a weapon of war, and large-scale plunder and murder are also occurring as part of efforts to displace people on resource-rich land.

Dirk Patton

The UN's current mission in the Democratic Republic of Congo, called MONUC, is entering its thirteenth year. MONUC is the UN's largest and longest-lasting mission to date. It is mandated to protect civilians and also help in the reconstruction of the country. With 18,000 people, MONUC is spread thinly across northeastern Congo and is largely unable to halt attacks. Rebels continue to kill and plunder natural resources with impunity. Some claim the rebels are supported by an international crime network stretching through Africa to Western Europe and North America.

The international community's support for political and diplomatic efforts to end the war has been relatively consistent, but no effective steps have been taken to abide by repeated pledges to demand accountability for the war crimes and crimes against humanity that are routinely committed in Congo. The United Nations Security Council and the U.N. Secretary-General have frequently denounced human rights abuses and the humanitarian disaster that the war unleashed on the local population. But they have shown little will to tackle the responsibility of occupying powers for the atrocities taking place in areas under their control, areas where the worst violence in the country took place.

Hunter's Rain is set early in the first days of the conflict. Before the international community and the UN had really taken notice. It is a fictionalized story based on some of the actual horrors that occurred in central Africa, and that are still occurring to this day. As you read, you will uncover some clues that shaped who John Chase is and foretold the coming of the V Plague virus. It is a stand-alone prequel to the V Plague series and does not fit in with the series timeline, rather only provides a bit more of John's backstory. The timing is before the events that brought about the infection and, ultimately, the apocalypse. It can be read at any point within the series.

That said, Hunter's Rain picks up where my short story, Rules Of Engagement, ends. If you have not read it yet, while not entirely necessary to enjoy this work, it will introduce you to some of the characters and situations.

Dirk Patton

Hunter's Rain

1

The condo was cramped, but at least it was in a good area of McLean, Virginia. If you stood in just the right spot and stretched your neck way to the left, you could catch a glimpse of the Potomac through the kitchen window. And, it was an easy commute to CIA headquarters. That was why Katie had bought it.

It was bright, clean and sparsely yet tastefully decorated. Fortunately, my new bride wasn't the fairy princess type so there wasn't pink frilly crap all over the place. But, if she had been, I'd have found a way to live with it. Dumping my heavy duffel bag on the floor near the stairs that led to the master bedroom, I stood there for a moment. Looking around. Taking the place in.

This was the first time I'd ever set foot in Katie's home, so I had to ask where the bathroom was. She pointed me up the stairs and went back to sorting through a thick stack of mail.

It had been over a month since she'd been home and the air was stale and musty. After availing myself of the facilities, I opened a set of French doors that led from the master bedroom onto a small balcony overlooking the parking lot.

Dirk Patton

We had just gotten back to Washington after a whirlwind vacation that culminated in a stop in Vegas. The ceremony had been memorable because the guy that officiated our wedding had been wearing a blue leisure suit straight out of 1975. He also had coal black hair, greased into a perfect ducktail that would have been the envy of every male in the 1950s. After he pronounced us man and wife, I half expected him to say "Thank you very much" in an impersonation of Elvis. But he didn't.

Katie and I hadn't met that long ago. Just a few weeks actually. It had been in a shithole Central American jungle. She was in the country at the behest of her employer, the Central Intelligence Agency, and things hadn't gone well. Somehow, a rebel commander, who bore a striking resemblance to the Frito Bandito, had found out who she was and taken her prisoner.

He was working with a group of Russian military advisors who were camped out deep in the jungle and had decided to deliver the pretty, young CIA agent to them as a gift. That was where I came in. My name is John Chase, and I'm a member of the US Army's Delta Force.

My unit had been inserted into that very same patch of jungle with orders to eliminate that very same rebel commander. Since the Russians had arrived, providing arms and training to his ragtag followers, the local government had been getting a bloody nose on a fairly regular basis. Mr. Bandito was well on his way to becoming a folk hero to the majority of the country's population, who were tired of living in stark poverty.

Can't say as I blame them for wanting a change, but inviting the Russians in is a little like hosting an open bar at a wedding reception. May sound good when you're planning it, but it's going to cost you more than you ever imagined in the end. Not that the US has a dramatically better track record, but my job wasn't to make policy. It was to carry out the orders of whatever politician happened to be in charge.

So El Presidente, growing concerned over the recent success of the rebels, expressed his fears to the local CIA station chief. He pointed out that if the rebels toppled him, the Russians would gain a foothold in America's backyard. The station chief did his job and got on the phone with Langley, who went running to the White House. POTUS lit a fire under the ass of the Chairman of the Joint Chiefs, who fired off a very unambiguous order from his office in the E Ring of the Pentagon. Shit kept rolling downhill until my unit was tasked with solving the problem. Permanently.

That's how I wound up hiding in a jungle in Central America, watching the most beautiful woman I'd ever seen as she was escorted into the

Russian commander's tent. Long story short, I'd completed my mission, rescued the girl and flown off into the sunset. Well, actually it was the sunrise, but sunset sounds so much more poetic.

It had been love at first sight, at least for me. We had been thoroughly debriefed on the aircraft carrier we were extracted to, then flown to Washington where Katie disappeared to a CIA safe house for several days of an intense mission post mortem. I went through the same thing with Army Intelligence (yes, I know, that's an oxymoron), a stone-faced CIA officer sitting in on the whole thing.

When it was all over, I pulled the CIA guy aside. Handing him a slip of paper with my phone number written on it, I asked him to give it to Katie. I didn't really expect to ever hear from or see her again, but six hours later my phone rang.

I had some leave coming. As it turned out, so did she. It took several conversations over the phone and more than a few drinks in a bar in Georgetown, but I eventually talked her into heading out on a road trip with me. From that point, things moved fast. Whirlwind fast, and I was still trying to wrap my head around the fact that I was married.

Going back down the stairs, I stepped over my duffel bag, which probably weighed more than my wife, and walked into the kitchen. She was finishing with her mail, junk sorted from stuff she actually needed or wanted. The toss pile was about ten times thicker. Sweeping it into the garbage, she placed the rest on a small desk and wrapped her arms around my neck, pressing her body tightly against me.

"Welcome home," she smiled and started to step back when the kiss ended.

But, she had awakened the beast, and I pulled her back against my chest. Soon our clothing started coming off and we stumbled towards the living room, collapsing onto the couch. Her panties came off with a tearing sound, and I was happy when she wasn't concerned over a pair of underwear being ruined by her brute of a husband.

Just before things really got interesting, the doorbell rang. A moment later there was a loud pounding on the window next to it. I looked over the back of the couch to see the grinning face of Mike Anderson, known as Spider, one of my teammates. I had completely forgotten that I'd given him the address. He was here to pick me up so we could report to the Pentagon for some unknown reason.

I had already learned that Katie was far from being a prude, but that didn't mean she was an exhibitionist. With a smile of regret, she had grabbed a lightweight blanket from the couch and covered herself. Grabbing up her scattered clothes, she made a dash for the stairs. Unaccustomed to anything being in the way, she wasn't paying attention and ran directly into my duffel.

It didn't budge, and I heard a snap as one of her toes broke. She fell backward into a chair, holding her foot up in the air and let loose with a stream of curses that damn near made *me* blush. The doorbell rang again and I shouted at Spider to hold his water.

Katie had broken the long toe next to the big one on her right foot, and it was at a severe angle. Tears wet her eyes from the pain and as I bent for a closer look, I expected to be torn to ribbons for having left my bag on the floor. But, she didn't say a word about that, just asked if I'd pop it back straight.

Apologizing profusely for having caused her injury, I did as she asked and set the broken digit as best I could. It didn't go straight, remaining at a very noticeable bend, but it must have eased the pain. As soon as I adjusted it, she leaned back and breathed a sigh of relief.

Despite my best efforts, she refused to go to the emergency room and get it treated properly. She explained that if she went to an ER, her name would get entered into their computers. About a minute later an alert would pop up at the CIA that one of their employees was at a hospital seeking medical attention.

There was a valid concern that, while under any form of sedation, a person might inadvertently reveal classified information. So a minute after that, an Agency officer would be dispatched to the hospital to ensure that national security wasn't compromised. Then there would be about an inch of paperwork. Katie wasn't going to deal with all that for a broken toe.

Wrapping the blanket tightly around her breasts, she'd stood and kissed me before limping up the stairs. I watched her all the way up, enjoying the way the blanket parted around her hips with each step. Stopping at the top, she told me to hurry the hell up at the Pentagon so we could pick up where we left off. With a spring in my step, I walked over and opened the front door to let Spider in.

"Dude! Really?" He said when he saw me.

I looked down, realizing I was as naked as a jaybird. I've been in the Army a long time, and one of the first things to go during basic training is modesty. You're in an open barrack with about fifty other guys. You shit, shower and change clothes with absolutely no privacy. It's a shock to the system at first, but you get used to it in a hurry and eventually don't even notice. But we weren't in the barracks. I'd just been more than a little distracted.

"Jealous?" I asked, bending to collect my clothes off the floor.

Spider is a large black man, and when I say large, I'm not just talking about his stature.

"Of that? Jesus Christ, how the hell does a woman even know when you're in?" He shot back, pointing at my dick.

I threw my underwear at him, but he ducked, and they sailed over his shoulder and wound up draped over a framed photo of Katie's mother.

"House rule number one. No underwear on my mother's picture."

We looked up to see Katie standing at the top of the stairs, a robe cinched tightly around her narrow waist. Spider snatched my briefs off the frame and hid them behind his back. Yes, that's what teammates do for each other.

"Ma'am," he said to Katie.

"Ma'am?" She looked at me. "Did you tell him?"

"Tell me what?" Spider looked at me.

Hunter's Rain

"We got married," I said, unable to keep myself from grinning like an idiot.

He grinned back, a moment later my underwear rocketing out of his hand and hitting me squarely in the face.

2

A couple of hours later, Spider and I drove through the gate and began looking for a spot in the massive Pentagon parking lot. I'd been here a couple of times before but was still awed by the sheer size of the building. We had passed through gate security, hardly even checked as both of us were wearing Class A uniforms, had the proper ID and were on the list for the day.

Neither of us was one bit happy about being ordered to a meeting at the Pentagon. We are covert operators, the key word there being *covert*. Showing up at the front door of one of the largest buildings in the world, that just so happens to house the entire senior command structure of the US military, is hardly covert. And to top it off, we come walking up in Class A's.

Not that there was any insignia that would reveal what we really were, but... two men in uniform that included green beret headgear. Plus, we were rarely in uniform, on or off post, so we didn't wear ours comfortably like the guys who did so on a daily basis. That just made us stand out even more.

Why did this matter? Because the US has a lot of enemies in the world. Some are ragged little fighters in shitty corners of the globe that live for the opportunity to kill an American. They aren't the ones I worry about. The ones that are truly dangerous are the professional spies and operators that work for governments that have a different agenda than our own.

It is not only likely, but it is also expected that foreign agents routinely photograph every person who enters and exits every US military installation in the world. Much of the time this is done by people on the ground with a long-lensed camera, but there's a lot that can be seen from orbit by spy satellites. Hell, we do it to them. It's very hard to stay hidden in today's world.

They look for patterns in people's movements. Catalog their images after running them through facial recognition software. Create or add to files that can be amazingly comprehensive and include startlingly accurate personal information. No, walking through the front door of the Pentagon was not something we should be doing. But orders are orders and, despite Spider's complaints when they'd been given to him, here we were.

"Well, that little Poindexter at the gate wouldn't know a bad guy if one bit him on the ass," Spider said, snapping me out of my musings as he steered away from a section that was marked as Officers Only. "We could have had half a dozen tangos stuffed in the trunk, armed to the teeth, and he wouldn't have noticed."

I turned and looked around the interior of his Corvette. Half a dozen terrorists in the trunk? Hell, the damn car was so tight the two of us had our shoulders wedged against each other just so we could close the doors.

"Yeah, well, fuck you. You know what I mean."

I hadn't even had to say anything.

"Any idea why we're here?" I asked as he raced to the end of a long row and wheeled into a vacant slot. We were probably about three hundred yards from the closest entrance.

"Nope. The Colonel called me early this morning and said to get my ass up here and collect you," he said, shutting down the rumbling engine and opening his door. "What did you do now?"

By *up here*, he meant he had been at Fort Bragg in North Carolina. That's where we were assigned to the Army's 1st Special Forces Operational Detachment – Delta. More commonly known as Delta Force. And, he was just busting my chops about being in trouble. If I'd done something wrong, which I hadn't, Colonel Williams wouldn't call me to the Pentagon to chew me out. He was quite capable of doing that at Bragg. As was

Command Sergeant Major Turner. I was still missing a large part of my ass from the last time I'd crossed that old warhorse.

"I'm not supposed to say anything," I said, lowering my voice. "I'm being promoted. I'm going to be an officer."

Spider stopped dead in his tracks, starting to open his mouth. He looked at me for half a second before a grin broke across my face.

"The day the Army makes you an officer, I'll resign and go join the Marines," he said, taking big strides to catch up with me.

"So it would be an all-around improvement for the Army, and a sad day for the Corps," I said, moving to the side in case he decided to hit me.

But, I was safe. We were approaching the entrance, and it was time to behave. Both of us wiped the smiles off our faces and did a quick check of our uniforms as we pushed through and came to a stop in the line for security. Spider nudged me, and I looked in the direction he nodded.

A Marine Sergeant, working the security detail, was checking us out. He glanced down at something on his desk, then stood and marched over to where we stood. We were sandwiched between a Navy Commander and an Air Force Captain, both of them women. They were both short, even for females, and just made us stick out that much more. The Marine had a clipboard in his hand and came to a stop, looking us up and down.

"Sergeant First Class Chase and Staff Sergeant Anderson?" He asked.

The Commander to our front looked over her shoulder and came face to face with Spider's chest. She took a couple of steps away from us.

"That's us, Sergeant," I said.

"If you'll follow me, I'll be your escort," he said, turning and marching towards another entrance door for which there was no line waiting.

Spider and I exchanged glances then fell in behind him. He paused at a security station which was manned by two Marines and asked for our ID cards. He swiped them through a card reader, handing them back along with a clip on badge for each of us that had a big, red V against a white background.

Even if you're in the military, you don't walk around the Pentagon without some type of visible ID badge. If you're assigned to the building, then it will be a permanent card with your photo. Otherwise, you're one of the Vs. It was taken very seriously, and I'd heard a story about an Air Force Colonel that had objected to being asked to wear the badge and dressed down the Marine guards working security.

According to the story, he was still yelling at the Marines when the Commandant of the Marine Corps, who works in the building, got wind of what was going on. A phone at the security station rang and within twenty seconds the Colonel found himself in handcuffs, being escorted to a holding cell by the Marine he had been yelling at. Thirty minutes later the Air Force Chief of Staff, who also works in the building, walked into the cell and informed the Colonel that the United States Air Force no longer required his services. He was allowed to retire, effective immediately.

There are a thousand more stories like that floating around the military. There's the poor Soldier who was suddenly demoted because a General didn't like the way he saluted. The Marine that was reassigned to guard an unmanned listening post in Alaska because he had accidentally bumped into an Admiral that was walking around a corner.

Ninety-nine percent of them are bullshit, but they all demonstrate how much the average Soldier, Sailor, Airman or Marine doesn't want to go anywhere near the place. There's enough brass (high ranking officers) to open a spittoon factory. And, where there's brass, there's a good chance one of them will notice you if you're not on your toes.

Or even if you are and they just don't like your looks. So if you haven't been ordered to report there, no one I know would touch it with a ten-foot pole.

The guard waited until each of us clipped the V badges to our uniform jackets, precisely in the prescribed location. Satisfied, he turned and nodded, and one of the Marines guarding a door swiped a key card. There was a thunk as a locking bolt retracted and we followed our escort into a narrow tunnel.

He marched like we were on a parade ground and I fought the impulse to imitate him. I had no doubt Spider was having the same internal struggle as he's even a bigger smart ass than I am.

We didn't go far before exiting into a plushly carpeted hallway and turned right. I glanced at the first door we passed in surprise. It was the office of the Secretary of Defense. The next door was only a few yards farther down the corridor. Four large men wearing dark suits and earpieces stood in front of it, watching us approach.

The Marine walked directly to one of them and gave him our names. He checked a clipboard before looking up and scrutinizing each of our faces. I caught a glimpse of a photo of Spider amongst the papers in his hand.

Hunter's Rain

"Gentlemen, are either of you armed?" He asked. We both nodded our heads.

He nodded at one of the other suits who came forward with two heavy bags with large, brass zippers. They looked very much like the kind of things a store owner with a lot of cash would use to go to the bank, only bigger.

"If you would each deposit your weapons in the bags, please. They will be returned to you when you're done."

Spider glanced at me, and I nodded that it was OK to comply with the request. Each of us removed a pistol, dropped the magazine and racked the slide to eject the live round in the chamber. Weapons empty, we deposited them into the bags. I added a four inch assisted opening folding knife and a Japanese Kubotan.

The Kubotan is a five-and-a-half-inch length of hardened Lexan, about half an inch thick with one blunt and one sharp end. Four compressed rings around the middle of the body perfectly fit four fingers, and when gripped in a fist it can cause serious damage to an attacker.

It was the last of my weapons, and another suit stepped up with a metal detecting wand and gestured for me to raise my arms. He scanned my front, then asked me to turn around before completing his check. When finished with me, he scanned Spider and stepped away, nodding to the man who seemed to be in charge of the security detail.

"Wait here, please," the man said, slipping quietly through the unmarked door behind him. A moment later he came back out, holding the door open with one hand.

"Gentlemen," he gestured for us to pass through the door.

I led the way and nearly came to a hard stop, but managed to maintain my composure and continue all the way into the large conference room. The Secretary of Defense, SECDEF, was seated at the end of the table closest to me. To his immediate right was General Kurtz, Chairman of the Joint Chiefs, then General Hillis, Commanding General of the Army. Colonel Williams, my CO, sat to SECDEF's left.

Everyone was looking at us, but other than noting their presence I was staring at the far end of the room. I recognized the Secretary of State from TV but hardly gave him a second glance. Seated at the head of the table, appearing even larger than he did on TV, was the President of the United States.

Spider and I both came to rigid attention. At most, I'd expected to be in a room with some senior officers, but nothing higher than a Colonel. In the Pentagon, Colonels are common folk. I sure as hell

Hunter's Rain

hadn't expected the President of the United States (POTUS) and several members of the senior military leadership of the country.

"Gentlemen," POTUS said, getting to his feet and striding swiftly around the table with his hand extended. "Thank you for joining us."

I cut my eyes toward the assembled brass, looking for some help. What the hell did I do? There are protocols for a service member who meets the President, but there's also a briefing that goes along with them so you don't do something wrong and look like an idiot. Did I salute? Did I shake the man's hand? General Kurtz saw my look and nodded as he surreptitiously made a shaking motion with his right hand. He'd left the other one behind in Vietnam.

Taking his cue, I extended my hand. POTUS took it and placed his other hand on my elbow as we shook. He repeated with Spider then took a step back.

"I understand congratulations are in order," he said to me with a big smile.

"Sir?" I asked, completely thrown by the whole situation.

"I believe you just got married?"

"Yes, sir. I did. Thank you, sir," I said, my brain beginning to work again, though sluggishly.

"I'm sure she's a lucky woman, young man. Treat her right, and you'll have a long, happy marriage."

There was a twinkle in his eye as he said this.

"Yes, sir, Mr. President. I intend to."

"Good! My wife is actually the reason I'm standing here right now. She has a dear friend that is doing some missionary work overseas. Her friend has brought some disturbing events to my attention, and I've asked the Secretary to see what can be done." He was referring to SECDEF. "With that, I'm off. I just wanted to congratulate you and wish you a healthy and happy life with your new bride."

"Thank you, Mr. President," I said as he shook my hand again.

With that he swept out of the room and for a moment I wasn't even sure what had just happened.

"He has that effect on people," SECDEF said, understanding what I was feeling. "Have a seat, and we'll get started."

3

When we came out of the conference room less than an hour later, our Marine escort was waiting for us. He handed over the bags with our weapons and took off, marching towards the door we'd come through earlier. We fell in behind him and were soon in the public lobby where he collected our V badges and checked us out of the building.

"What do we do with the bags?" Spider asked him. We hadn't reloaded our weapons standing in the middle of the Pentagon's E Ring hallway.

"Beats me," he said. "They belong to the Secret Service, but they left with POTUS. Guess you keep them."

Spider nodded, and we exited into the fresh evening air. Washington DC is not one of my favorite places, especially in the summer. It's hot, humid, crowded and it always seems as if there's someone keeping an eye on you if you're in uniform. It kind of feels like being under the microscope all the time, and I was happy that we were on our way to Fort Bragg.

Well, not happy that I was leaving Katie already, but glad that I wasn't going to be sticking around the nation's capital. That was a feeling I was going to have to do something about. My wife worked in the damn city. Well, she had an office here. She worked wherever the Agency needed her, but in reality, the majority of her time was spent at Langley.

Reaching Spider's car, we took a moment to load our weapons and rearm ourselves. The bags were tossed behind the front seat then we squeezed inside. It took a few minutes to make our way out of the parking lot, passing through security and accelerating onto I-395.

"Now just what the fuck was that?" Spider asked once we were up to speed and weaving through the heavy traffic on our way to Katie's condo. "Since when does POTUS and the top brass take time to brief two lowly Delta troopers?"

"Beats the hell out of me," I said. "But I've got a feeling there's a lot more going on behind the scenes than we were told. POTUS doesn't come to the Pentagon, the Pentagon comes to him."

Spider grunted and nodded, waiting until it was almost too late to take the exit he needed. Without bothering to look, he nailed the throttle, whipped the car across three lanes of traffic and onto the off ramp. Horns blared, and there was a screeching of tires, but thankfully no crunches of metal on metal.

Hunter's Rain

"Can we get there in one piece?" I shouted.

I'm not a good passenger, and I freely admit it. I've been accused of being a control freak and not being able to stand to relinquish even the steering wheel to anyone else. That's just not true. I simply know that I'm a better driver than everyone else.

"Pussy," he muttered, accelerating to beat the light at the bottom of the ramp.

Some time later, I was too nervous to look at my watch, we pulled into the parking lot at Katie's condo. Spider wheeled into a reserved spot and shut the engine off.

"I'll wait here in case you want to say a proper goodbye," he grinned. "Shouldn't take very long, knowing you."

I flipped him off and unfolded myself out of the car. He climbed out the other side and opened the small cargo hatch and grabbed some clothes.

"You're not changing in my wife's parking lot," I said as he began unbuttoning his uniform jacket. He paused and gave me an innocent look.

"Why not?"

"Jesus Christ, Spider. You're going to cause me to get divorced before she has a chance to get tired of me. Come inside and change."

I lead the way, knocking on the door when we got there. Katie hadn't had time to give me a key, and everything with her was so new I'm not sure I would have felt comfortable just walking in if I even had one. She opened the door quickly, smiling when she saw us. As I stepped across the threshold, she pulled me close and kissed me.

"How did the meeting go?" She asked as Spider disappeared into the guest bath to change out of his Class A.

"A little unusual," I said. "I've got to go to work. We're leaving as soon as we change clothes."

Her face creased for a moment, then the smile returned, and she threw her arms around my neck.

"How long?" She asked, wanting to know when I'd be back.

"I don't know," I answered truthfully. "I just got the dog and pony show from the brass as they impressed upon us how important this was. The real brief will be when I get back to Bragg."

"You know my security clearance is even higher than yours," she whispered in my ear, wanting details.

"Then you know what would happen to me if I told you anything that you didn't have a need to know," I whispered back, holding her tight and letting my hands drift down to squeeze her ass.

"Never mind the large, black man in the room," Spider said when he came out of the bath and saw where my hands were. He was doing his best Will Smith impersonation.

"I never mind that," Katie shot right back with a wicked little grin, gave me a quick kiss and headed up the stairs.

Spider and I stared at each other for a moment, our mouths hanging open in surprise, then he roared with laughter.

"Oh, she's a keeper," he laughed.

"Get the fuck out of my house," I said, beginning to undress.

4

It's about a four-and-a-half-hour drive from DC to Fort Bragg in North Carolina. From Washington, you head south on Interstate 95, then go west for a few miles on I-295 a little north of Fayetteville. Spider had driven because it takes about the same amount of time to screw with a commercial flight and an airport on each end, and driving is a whole lot less hassle. He'd checked to see if there were any military flights going to Andrews Air Force Base, but nothing that would have worked out with the timing of our meeting.

Rolling up to the main gate at Bragg, he passed our IDs over to the civilian contractor security guard. Soldiers were present, making sure no one forced their way onto post, but it was the contractor's job to properly clear anyone wanting access to the sprawling installation. It took a few minutes, then he hit a button to raise a gate and waved us through.

It was the middle of the night, but like any large military base there were a lot of people up and moving. We wound up sandwiched between two deuce and a halfs loaded with soldiers from the 82nd Airborne, which is also based at Bragg. They made a turn onto the road that would take them to Pope Air Force Base. Watching, I idly wondered where the politicians were sending them.

Hunter's Rain

Spider drove carefully and slightly below the posted speed limit. A speeding ticket in the civilian world is a minor annoyance. On an Army post? Well, let's put it this way. I'd rather spend a week at the proctologist's office and top it off with a Bette Midler concert.

We drove for a long time. Fort Bragg is large, something like two hundred and fifty square miles and the compound reserved for Delta is far removed from the day-to-day activities of the base. We drove on through the dark, having left the last sign of civilization behind several minutes ago. Turning onto a small, unmarked road, we drove through a tunnel of trees, made another sharp turn and came to a stop at an unlit security checkpoint.

No civilian contractor here. This was the entrance into Delta's area, which is more of a fort within the fort. An Army MP Staff Sergeant, wearing night vision, stepped to the car. There would be four other MPs, armed with heavy weapons, keeping an eye on us from hardened defensive points.

We knew the guard, and he knew us by sight, but still asked for our IDs and checked them as carefully as if we were complete strangers. It only took a few moments before he handed them back and opened the outer of two gates. Spider drove forward and stopped, waiting for the outer gate to close. When it did, the inner gate opened, and we were free to proceed.

We drove for several more minutes, passing numerous training buildings before reaching the main barracks we worked out of, and sometimes lived in. It was simply labeled *Squadron B*, with no other indication of what it was or whom it housed. Parking, we climbed out and walked through the front door.

A large, well-lit space greeted us. The walls were covered with more photos of men fighting in various places around the world than I'd ever had time to look at. A large floor to ceiling plaque dominated the wall directly to our front. It was almost half full of small, brass plates into which a rank, name and date were engraved. Men who had given their all and hadn't come home.

Spider pushed through a heavy door to our right, and we entered another large area we just called the clubhouse. There were several mismatched sofas and chairs scattered around, oriented towards a large TV. Beyond, a spacious kitchen with three large refrigerators and a big, round table with ten chairs spaced around it. An open doorway led into a long hallway with eight small rooms set up with bunks.

Painted on the wall behind the TV was an impressive mural of five grim reapers. They were approaching through a dark forest, each of them with an M16 in their hand rather than the traditional scythe. The one in the lead carried a severed human head in his other hand, holding it forward and grinning a skeletal grin. My small team had been dubbed the *Reapers* several years ago and one of our shooters, who was just as talented with paint and brush as he was with a gun, spent two long months creating the mural.

A medium sized man with shaggy hair and wispy beard sat on one of the sofas watching TV, looking up when we walked in. Poon-tang, our resident sniper. He wasn't a big talker, preferring to let his Barrett rifle speak for him.

"Miss me?" Spider shouted, jumping over the back of the couch and landing on the cushion next to Poon. He tried to wrap the smaller man up and kiss the top of his head, which he knew Poon absolutely hated. He got a sharp elbow in his solar plexus and a hand in the face to halt his smacking lips.

"You two need a room?" I asked, dumping my duffel on the floor.

"You hear about Jim?" Poon asked when Spider gave up and moved to the far end of the sofa.

Master Sergeant Jim Hicks, our team leader, had broken his leg a few weeks ago when he stepped in an unseen hole in a Central American jungle. The doctors had to put in two plates and a bunch of screws to repair the bone. He was waiting to see if it would heal properly and he'd be able to come back to Delta.

I shook my head and dropped into a worn recliner.

"What? His leg?"

"Yeah. Doc said it wasn't healing right and he's going back into surgery this morning. Doesn't look like he'll be coming back," Poon said, turning his attention back to the TV.

We were all quiet for a while, even Spider, which is very unusual. Getting hurt or killed is a very real possibility in our line of work, but not something we worry about. You can't, or you'd wind up paralyzed with fear. But of the two, getting hurt badly enough to have to give up your slot in Delta, and maybe even be forced into medical retirement from the Army, would be the worst.

What the hell else would I do? I've been in uniform since the day after I graduated from High School. I really don't know anything else. I'm not a kid anymore and knew the day would come when my body couldn't continue to endure the torture of life as a Special Forces Operator, but I hoped that day was a long way off.

Hunter's Rain

"How's he doing?" I meant his mental attitude.

"Not good," Poon said, turning to look at me with hooded eyes. "This is pretty fucked up. Could have happened to any of us. Step in a goddamn hole and break your leg and you're done. Go sit in a shitty apartment, eat TV dinners and watch Oprah all fucking day. No thanks. I'll stick my gun in my mouth first."

He had just expressed how we all thought, but it was still sobering to hear it. Never one to let a moment get too maudlin, Spider jumped up and went to the kitchen. He returned with three cold bottles of beer and passed them out.

"To Jim, and to Bubba," he said, still standing and holding his bottle up. We raised ours and drank deeply.

Bubba was the other member of our team who was missing. He hadn't come back from the mission in Central America where Jim had broken his leg. A Russian bullet to the head had ended his life. His body had toppled into a fast running stream and been washed away, which had been a blessing in disguise.

If we had been able to recover his body when he'd been killed, none of us would be here today. We'd been chased through miles of thick jungle by some very pissed off Spetsnaz and their dogs, barely getting away. The weight of a body would have slowed us down, and we wouldn't have made our extraction.

Once we'd reached the aircraft carrier, steaming in the Caribbean, I'd convinced the Captain to help me find and recover Bubba's body. None of us were going to go back home without him. With the Navy's help, we finally spotted the corpse of our brother by using a satellite feed from the National Reconnaissance Office.

Bubba had been washed seventeen miles downstream into a larger river where his body had beached on a sandbar. Poon, Spider and I had taken a fast ride on a Navy helo and recovered Bubba's remains. He was laid to rest at Arlington National Cemetery three days later.

"So how was the fancy dress ball?" Poon asked after he drained his beer.

"A ball would have been more fun," I said.

"We met POTUS," Spider chimed in.

"You are so full of shit. I'd slap you, but you'd probably splatter all over the room," Poon said, glaring at Spider's grinning face. When the grin didn't change, he looked at me and I nodded.

"No fuckin' way," he said, looking back and forth between us. "What the hell was he doing there?"

"We got there a little early, and he was still in the room. He shook our hands and left, then we got the usual speeches about how important this mission is. The Colonel will be in later in the morning to brief us. Don't know much more than that."

"So where are we going?" Poon asked, clicking the TV remote to shut it off.

"Africa," I said, dropped my empty beer bottle in a trashcan and headed down the hall to get some sleep.

5

Five hours later I grabbed for my pistol when a god-awful banging woke me from a sound sleep. It took a couple of seconds to remember where I was. Rolling over in bed, I sighed and looked at the door shaking in its frame.

"What?" I shouted.

"Wakey wakey, eggs and bakey," Spider shouted back, thankfully ceasing his assault on the door. "And the Colonel called. He'll be here in thirty."

"Go the fuck away!" I shouted back, briefly considering sending a couple of rounds through the wall next to the door. Groaning, I sat up on the edge of the thin mattress.

Taking a deep breath, I stood, then dropped to the floor and started doing push-ups. I didn't count, just kept going until my arms were shaking and sweat was dripping off my nose onto the wooden floor. Grabbing a towel, I went down the hall and showered quickly, then went back to my room and dressed. Cargo pants and a polo shirt, if it matters.

Colonel Williams had arrived while I was getting cleaned up. He was a compact man with closely cropped hair and was always immaculately groomed and turned out. As much as we all looked like dirtbags, he was recruiting poster perfect. Three new faces sat at the table with him, each of them with a plate of the big breakfast Poon had prepared in front of them.

Two of them were operators I knew well from Squadron A, and I suspected they were replacements for Jim and Bubba. They stood and shook hands with me when I walked into the room. The third was an Army Captain in uniform, and I was surprised to see insignia for the Medical Corps. I filled a cup with coffee that smelled strong enough to peel paint, accepted a plate of food from Poon and took a seat at the table.

"Colonel," I greeted my CO as I took a sip from the cup. I was right about how strong it was.

"Good morning, Master Sergeant," he said. "Good leave I expect?"

"Yes, sir. It..." Master Sergeant? What the hell?

"Congratulations," he said, smiling as he pushed a new rank insignia and some papers across the table. "You're the new leader of Reaper Team."

I looked down at the paperwork and Master Sergeant's chevrons with mixed emotions. I was happy to be promoted and given command of the team, but it was at the expense of Jim Hicks, who was in surgery at the moment. The Colonel must have read the look on my face.

"He's not coming back," Williams said. "I talked to the doctors this morning. He'll be fine, but he's got a long road ahead just to walk normally again."

I nodded and thanked the Colonel. Moving the papers to the side, I dug into my breakfast as he began our briefing.

"Africa," the Colonel said clicking a button on a small remote that controlled a laptop connected to the TV. It had been turned so it was easily visible from the table.

The screen flared, a map filling the view. He clicked another button, zooming onto a region near the center of the continent and just barely south of the equator. The whole area was broken up by dotted lines, looking like a jigsaw puzzle with dozens of tiny pieces.

"We've been watching this region deteriorate into chaos for the past several months. There's currently discussion in the UN about sending in peacekeepers. It's bad, and getting worse. The warlords are seizing all humanitarian shipments that are making it into the area. The people are starving. Quite literally to death.

Hunter's Rain

"The first lady received a call late last week from a childhood friend who is a missionary and aid worker in the area. She was in trouble, and a SEAL team extracted her about an hour before the compound where she was hiding was raided by one of the warlords. When she told the first lady about what was happening and what she had seen... well, let's just say that POTUS has taken a personal interest.

"Each of these little chunks of land is a territory claimed by a specific warlord. That's why you're going in. Officially a pacification mission. There's already an Aussie SASR (Special Air Service Regiment) team on the ground. POTUS has spoken with the Australian PM, and they're happy to have us join the party. They've been in-country for almost a month, and while they're doing some good, they can do more with some help.

"There's two local CIA assets that will be providing intel to a case officer that will link up with you before you're in-country. You'll operate with the Australians and will have operational command of the mission. Everything is in your briefing packets."

He gestured at a spot on the kitchen counter where several thick binders sat waiting for us.

"Go through the packets today, and we'll talk more tomorrow morning. Questions?" He sipped his coffee and leaned back in his chair and lit a cigarette.

It wasn't much of a briefing, but that's the way it normally is. We're big boys in Delta. We don't need every little detail read to us. When the Colonel left, we'd each grab a packet and go through it carefully. Tomorrow morning would be a much more involved and detailed conversation. But I had questions I wanted answered right away.

"Several, sir," I said, pushing my empty plate away. "First, you said this is "officially" a pacification mission. That means there's an "unofficial" part. What's going on?"

He nodded at the Medical Corp Captain. "That's why he's going along with you."

"Excuse me?" I didn't like the idea of a non-combatant tagging along. Not one bit. He would be a burden that could easily compromise our mission.

"Captain, if you would?" The Colonel turned to him.

The man was nervous, and it showed. He was thin, almost painfully so, with soft, pink skin. He spent his time indoors in air conditioning, with clean water and hot food and pleasant latrines. What the hell was the Colonel thinking, sending this man into the field?

Hunter's Rain

"My name is Captain Channing, and I'm from USAMRIID," he said, instantly getting our attention.

The US Army Medical Research Institute for Infectious Diseases dealt with the nastiest bugs on the planet. Things like the common cold or even the flu didn't get their attention. Ebola, Hantavirus, Machupo, Bubonic Plague, Anthrax and more that I couldn't think of off the top of my head, did. These were the diseases of nightmares that they worked on and tried to make sure we were prepared for the day when some asshole weaponized one of them and turned it loose in the world. I didn't like this one bit.

"Intelligence has been received that there are currently efforts underway in this region to collect viral samples from various species of primates. I cannot share any specifics about the type of virus that is being sought, but we do know the geographical area that is being targeted. If we are able to intercept any of the personnel involved in the sampling, I will be able to test the material they are collecting. We are hopeful this will help us prepare for whatever they are trying to develop."

"Why can't we just bring you some samples?" Poon-tang asked.

"You would potentially be at significant risk of contracting the virus. And we certainly do not want it transported back to the United States. It is better to take it to an appropriately equipped laboratory that is not within our borders."

"Fuck me," Spider breathed.

"There are more details in your briefing packets," the Captain said. "I will be available to answer any of your questions once you've read them."

The room was so silent you could have heard a mouse fart in the walls.

"You had another question, Master Sergeant?" The Colonel asked.

"Not at this time, sir," I said, completely creeped out by the thought of heading into a region where a bioweapon was being made.

6

Five days later I stood on the tarmac at Royal Australian Air Force (RAAF) Base Learmonth, on the northwestern corner of the island continent. It was going to be a long hop across the Indian Ocean to Africa, and thankfully the last leg of our trip. The weather was hot, a strong wind bringing the smell of the sea. My team was busily double-checking our gear and helping a very nervous Captain Channing get ready.

The last several days had been a whirlwind of activity with little time for sleep. I'd caught up on my sack time on the long flight to Australia. I was well rested at the moment and knew this was the best I'd be until we were back at Fort Bragg.

Each of us had read the briefing packets individually, then sat down as a team and discussed them at length. This helped cement details in our minds but was also effective at making sure everyone had picked up on the important bits of information they contained. One thing about briefing packets, they are thick because they contain a lot of extraneous bullshit. Sometimes, finding the gems amongst all that is a little like picking fly shit out of black pepper with boxing gloves on your hands.

Dirk Patton

I called a halt to the review around mid-afternoon, and we all headed to the range and kill house. There were two new team members, and a doctor tagging along on this mission. I wanted everyone to have as much time engaged in live fire exercises as possible. Our two new teammates were experienced troopers, and I had trained with them before, but they needed to get comfortable with us and vice versa.

Nitro was the older of the two. He was from Puerto Rico and built like a squat bulldog. He wore his hair long and his facial hair longer. If he didn't have arms like Arnold, he could have easily been mistaken for the actor Danny Trejo. He had to be one of the most intimidating looking men I'd ever seen, but once you got past the rough exterior he had a heart of gold and was a bigger joker than even Spider.

Two Step was from my home state of Texas. He favored Wrangler jeans and cowboy hats and was thin and spring steel hard. His favorite trick to impress women was to grab on to a pole, such as a streetlight, and lift himself until he was horizontal. I've seen him hold that pose for almost a minute. I tried it once and almost wound up in the hospital. Pound for pound, he was probably the strongest human being I'd ever met.

We'd spent a long afternoon with our weapons. I'd asked Poon to take the doctor under his wing and refresh everything the man had been taught in OCS (Officer Candidate School, or Organized Chicken Shit, depending on your perspective) about how to handle a weapon. To his credit, the man was a quick study and paid close attention to the lessons. Within a couple of hours, Poon had him reliably punching targets at three hundred yards.

Then we moved to the kill house. It is exactly what it sounds like. A house, only without a roof, where we practice killing. There are rooms and doors and rough wooden furniture that will hold up to the harsh North Carolina weather. Targets made to resemble people are strategically placed throughout. Some of them are static, and some are controlled by a spring system that will make them pop out at you when you enter a room. Some are obviously bad guys, some are obviously non-combatants and some you have to make a split-second decision and hope you're right.

The reason for no roof is the walls can be moved to reconfigure the floor plan. I figured it was time for a new layout, so I left the range ahead of the rest of the team and spent half an hour setting up a house none of them were familiar with. Targets got moved, and I was sitting on the hood of my truck when they pulled up.

There is a much more sophisticated indoor facility where the lighting can be controlled, and cameras record every angle of the action for later review and training. Range masters control reactive targets and can introduce new obstacles with the press of a button. Several different structures as well as buses, subway cars, even wide-body jet fuselages are housed inside the massive building. But I didn't need sophisticated training for the doctor. I just needed to pop his cherry a little.

Captain Channing was given a rifle without any ammo, or even a firing pin for that matter, and told to stay tight on Spider's back. He was getting a crash course on how to move with the team when it was time to shoot and scoot. Spider spent ten minutes instructing him on how to hold his weapon, what to do as the team moved, and how to be safe.

Fifteen seconds into the first exercise we had cleared two rooms, each target that needed shooting having been properly shredded when Spider called a halt. Turning, he unleashed verbal hell on the Captain who had run into his back, the muzzle of his weapon pressing into Spider's kidney.

Spider was about ten inches taller and eighty pounds heavier than the doctor, leaning down into his face and reading him the riot act. And act it was, though a necessary one. Spider was in fine form as he lit into the Captain. The doctor was about to shit his pants, but the rest of us lost it when Spider started quoting lines from Full Metal Jacket.

It was time for a good cop to step in, so I went over and pulled the doctor aside and spent a minute with him making sure he had gotten the concepts that had been screamed in his face. He surprised me when he recited them, almost verbatim, and said he was ready to go again. I nodded and told him to form back up on Spider.

We restarted, this time making it to the fourth room before he stepped directly into Nitro's firing lane. It was his good fortune that we were expecting him to make mistakes and were on high alert for just such an error. Spider tore into him again.

Third time we made it to the last room before the doctor tripped over Poon-tang's boot and fell flat on his face. Another round of yelling. The Captain took it all in stride, and the man continued to impress me, and I could tell the other guys were as surprised as I was. Between his appearance, and the Medical Corp insignia, we'd expected someone that would fold the first time Spider got in his face. We were wrong.

I reset walls, furniture and targets and we did it again. And again. Another re-configuration and we did it again. By now, the doctor was doing at least as well as anyone else on their first introduction to a kill house, and I was actually proud of the man. He was smart, and he was taking this very seriously and working hard. Sending everyone outside, I did a final reset of a couple of walls and added in what we called our initiator.

The initiator is a spring-loaded sweeper arm that will hit you with enough force to knock the wind out of your lungs and put you on your ass. I set it up in the fourth room, hidden just inside the left edge of the door so that as you stepped into the doorway it would trip and slam into your gut.

We started again, me in the lead. Sweeping through the first three rooms, I was pleased to see the Captain staying right with us. He was watching his areas just like he was supposed to, and making sure he didn't step into anyone's line of fire. He almost looked like a real Delta trooper.

Freezing the team with a raised, clenched fist, I motioned that I wanted the doctor to take the lead into the fourth room. He nodded and tapped Spider to let him know he was moving past him, then stepped towards the doorway. Everyone knew what was coming and relaxed, watching and waiting. All except Spider, who had to move with him so he didn't get suspicious.

He paused at the door, looking through at an angle like he'd been taught. Spider rolled across him to take the other angle and nodded an OK to go.

Hunter's Rain

Captain Channing rushed into the doorway and tripped the sensor on the initiator. The arm released and slammed around, striking him solidly right in the stomach and sending him flying five feet back into the room to land on his back.

Lying there, he looked up at us as we gathered around him, waiting for Spider to start yelling at him again. We all glared at him for a moment until he started squirming a little. With a grin and a laugh, Spider leaned down, grabbed his hand and pulled him to his feet. He stood there, looking around at our smiling faces, unsure what was happening.

"Relax, Doc," I said. "You just met the initiator. We all have, and every one of us wound up on our ass, just like you. Hell, tough guy here started crying."

I was pointing at Spider who took great exception to my comment.

"I wasn't crying, goddamn it! I had something in my eye, and it was watering. How many fuckin times do I have to tell you that?" He shouted in protest.

"Read Shakespeare, Doc?" Nitro chimed in. "What's the line about protesting too much?"

"Say I was crying again! Say I was crying again! I dare you! I double dare you, motherfucker.

Say I was crying one more goddamn time!" Spider shouted.

The rest of us lost it, and I thought Doc was going to pee his pants until he realized Spider was just being Spider and wasn't really upset. Still laughing, we grabbed brooms and cleaned up our brass and the debris from the targets we'd killed. When that was done, we headed for the widow maker.

The sun was setting as we started up the path that led to the tallest, steepest mountain on post. The trail was narrow and wound around for over a mile as we climbed the base, then eight hundred yards up a slope that was so severe you had to take most of it on all fours. Poon held the record for the fastest climb, and he set the pace.

I knew the rest of us could stay with him until we hit the steepest part of the trail, then he'd pull ahead and be standing at the summit when we arrived. Doc stayed with us, running easily on the lower slopes. Then the trail made a sharp jog to the left and started straight up, cutting through a narrow break in the rocks.

This was where Poon lightly sprang from spot to spot, opening his lead while the rest of us scrambled up the rough terrain. Doc didn't slow. He emulated Poon's leaps and stayed right on his ass. Within a few minutes, they reached the top, Doc only a couple of steps behind Poon.

The rest of us arrived as a group almost five minutes later. Doc stood next to Poon, watching us and doing his damnedest not to break into a shit-eating grin.

"Christ," Spider panted. "You're full of surprises, Doc."

"Been running marathons, hiking and rock climbing since I was in junior high," he grinned. "This felt great. It's good to get out of the lab."

"Alright, ladies. Let's get some chow and then take Doc out for some real fun," I said, starting my slipping, sliding way back down the mountain.

"What are we going to do?" Doc asked, appearing next to me and moving easier than I was.

"Ever jumped out of a perfectly good airplane?" I asked with a grin.

7

The plane droned as we made our way across the Indian Ocean. We were in the belly of an RAAF C-130 that had markings to make it look like a humanitarian aid flight. Actually, it was. We were crammed in amongst several large pallets of food and basic medical supplies. Each of us was stretched out, getting some rest before our arrival in Africa. Everyone but Doc, that is.

He hadn't been in a combat zone before. Hadn't jumped into a dark jungle that if the locals didn't kill you, the wildlife would make a valiant effort. He was as nervous as a virgin on prom night, sitting in a web sling seat and trying to read a book about the end of the world. Something to do with infected people chasing a small group of survivors, and their dog, all over America.

I ignored him and rolled onto my side, hoping to get a few hours of sleep before time to take a walk off the aircraft's rear ramp. We were jumping, our LZ a particularly remote area of the region. If all went according to plan, the Aussies would be waiting for us. I was looking forward to seeing their team leader, Staff Sergeant Lucas Martin.

Lucas and I had met at the British SAS barracks in Hereford, England. We had endured a mind-numbing conference for three days before getting to grab our packs and rifles and go have some fun in the English and Welsh countryside. We'd traded an occasional phone call since, but hadn't seen each other since parting ways at RAF Mildenhall. I had been headed to a shithole country with a lot of sand and camels and didn't know where he was going.

"Watch it, jackass."

I looked up to see Nitro rolling over as our other passenger made his way towards the cockpit. His name was Evan Delker, and he worked for the CIA. He was along to be the middleman between the Agency's local assets and us. I had briefly protested his inclusion, but Colonel Williams told me to shut up and deal with it. The powers that be had decided we couldn't be trusted to work directly with the CIA's assets, and they needed a presence on the ground to make sure everything went smoothly.

Translated, that meant some political wonk in Langley got wind that POTUS was personally interested in this operation and made sure the spooks were involved. Their assets, so we had to play nice if we wanted access to the intel. I've dealt with this shit before.

If things go well, the Agency runs around and whispers how they made sure the Army was well informed and advised. If things go FUBAR, then the whisperers say the Army refused to listen to their intel and advice. Either way, they win. Assholes.

Delker had been waiting for us in Australia. We'd arrived on a US Air Force jet in the middle of the night. At least it was dark there. It was the middle of the day for us. We were well rested after sleeping on the long flight that had originated at Pope Air Force Base with stops for fuel in California and Guam before the final run to the land down under. I'd found him in a secluded area of the air base, sitting in front of the barracks we would use for the next ten hours until our flight to Africa. He was smoking a cigar and drinking something over ice from a highball glass.

I'd walked up to introduce myself, slightly put off when he couldn't even stand up or take the fucking drink out of his hand long enough to shake. He was wearing khakis and a flowered Hawaiian shirt with a straw hat on his head. A few years my senior, he sat there looking me up and down like I was something he'd just stepped in and couldn't figure out how to get it off his shoe without touching it.

He'd only grunted when I'd introduced myself, so rather than yanking him out of the chair and instructing him on how to properly greet a stranger, I opted for diplomacy and walked into the barracks to make sure my team was getting settled. I wasn't surprised to see that Poon had taken to Doc and was sharing a room with him. Not often you see an officer share quarters with a Staff Sergeant, but the divisions of rank aren't nearly as rigid in the Special Forces.

"What's with Elliot Ness out there," Spider asked, hooking a thumb over his shoulder.

"Elliot Ness was FBI, moron," Nitro said as he dumped his gear on a narrow bunk.

Spider thought about that for a moment before flipping the other man off. Nitro just grinned and flexed.

"World's full of assholes," I said. "Figures we'd draw one. We'll see how he does at thirty thousand feet when the door opens."

"He'll shit his pressed khakis," Two Step chimed in.

"Don't count on it, pretty boy. You were still sucking your momma's tit when I went through BUDS."

Delker had come into the barracks and walked up behind us without anyone noticing.

"SEAL, huh?" I asked, turning and making a production of looking behind him.

"What are you doing?" He finally asked, irritation plain in his voice and on his face.

"Looking for a film crew," I met his angry glare and grinned. "Didn't think a SEAL could take a shit without making a media opportunity out of it."

A storm cloud crossed his face and he took a step forward. I grinned bigger, knowing I'd gotten under his skin, and squared my shoulders to face him. He stood there glaring for almost half a minute before breaking eye contact and shaking his head.

"You're as big of an asshole as I heard," he said.

"But you just met me. I'll grow on you," I said. "Now, do you want to have a civil conversation or shall we step outside?"

The grin had disappeared off my face at this point.

"We're going to be in the middle of a fucking jungle in a few hours, and if you and I are going to have a problem, let's have it now and get it out of the way."

I took a step into his personal space and looked down into his eyes. He stared right back, and I could see the animosity, but had no clue what

I'd done to offend this guy. We'd only just met, and I'd been on my best behavior. I hadn't said anything about his ugly shirt or stupid looking hat. I'd really had to bite my tongue not to comment on the loafers without socks.

Finally, he blinked and nodded. Moving back, he gestured down the hall where a cramped common area held a small table and half a dozen chairs. I stepped aside to let him lead the way, and the rest of us followed and took seats.

Delker had retired from the Navy to accept a position with the CIA. He had been in Africa for the past five years, developing and running intelligence assets from among the locals. He knew the region we were going into. Knew all the players in the constantly shifting power structure, and had eyes and ears in a lot of the warlord camps.

He had two assets, in particular, that were locals involved in the illegal arms and drug trade. They kept him informed on what each warlord was buying and selling and to whom. In exchange, I'm sure he did something for them that would be highly frowned upon back home, but was how business got done in third world countries. I didn't ask and didn't want to know. It's not unheard of for a member of the military to be called into a secret congressional committee hearing, and the less I knew about how the CIA operated in the region, the better.

Normally he would have stayed in Africa and linked up with us once we were on the ground, but things weren't normal. There were a couple of warlords that were tightening their hold in the area, and there were rumors about Chinese agents skulking around. The Chinese? What the hell did they want here? There was concern that he might be tracked and lead a problem right to us.

He briefed us for close to two hours, answering questions when we had them, but I didn't believe for a moment that his answers were complete, or even truthful. With a start, I realized I'd better adjust my attitude about CIA officers since I was now married to one. All I needed was to start doubting Katie and my new marriage would end badly.

8

Night had fallen when we reached Africa's east coast. That was fine with me. We were making a HALO (High Altitude Low Opening) insertion, and though there wouldn't be canopies that could be spotted until we were close to the ground, it's always easier to remain unseen in the dark. We were an hour from our jump point when the team began preparing.

Polypropylene thermal underwear went on first to protect us from the sub-zero temperatures we would encounter when we bailed out of the aircraft at slightly over thirty thousand feet. Our target on the ground was a sub-tropical mountainous area, but we had opted to come down on flatter, more open terrain and walk in.

The base elevation where we would touch down was thirty-three hundred and fifty feet above sea level and I'd already made sure everyone had their altimeters set correctly. Screw up that little detail and you were guaranteed to have a bad day. Nothing like the ground showing up a few hundred feet earlier than expected.

Doc was understandably nervous, breathing fast and sweating despite the cool air in the C-130. Poon helped him don the underwear and jumpsuit, getting his gear situated and speaking calmly to him. He had gotten half a dozen jumps in with us before we left Bragg, and I'd managed to snag a ride with him on a HALO training exercise for one of the other squadrons.

So, he wasn't a virgin, but he wasn't a veteran by any means. Poon had volunteered to be his jump buddy and would do everything he could to make sure it came off smoothly. Doc was hanging on his every word, smart enough to know his life depended on paying attention and not fucking up.

As each of us finished dressing, we secured masks on our lower faces and plugged into the plane's supply of pure oxygen. We would pre-breathe until just before jump time when we'd transition to portable O2 bottles for the fall to Earth. This would purge the nitrogen from our bloodstream so the rapid pressure change of falling six miles didn't cause it to turn gaseous and form bubbles that would lodge in our joints. The bends.

Painful as hell, so I'm told. Painful enough that it can distract a jumper so that he makes a mistake and winds up digging a grave with his body when he augers into the ground because he couldn't open his chute. Checking to make sure everyone was plugged into the oxygen, with their masks properly sealed against their faces, I sat back and relaxed.

Hunter's Rain

I had shaved my head before leaving Bragg, not wanting to go into an insect-infested jungle with a perfect hiding place for the little buggers. The skin that had been covered by hair was pale and itched like crazy. Tough guy that I am, I managed to deal with the discomfort.

As I sat and breathed in the slightly metallic tasting air, I thought about the mission. The region was rapidly ramping up to full-scale genocide. The UN was talking about putting troops on the ground, and the reports coming out of the country we were headed for were not good. Fifty thousand deaths in the past week. Men, women, children, families. And it was all spurred by generations old, tribal hatred. Those in power hated those that wanted to at least have a voice in how their country was governed. Instead of listening to the people, the political leadership decided to silence the dissent. Permanently.

Warlords were pawns of the government, allowed to do whatever they wished, as long as it was directed at the undesirable tribe, and many times at anyone at all. The aid that the UN was sending wasn't making it to the people who so desperately needed it. It was routinely being seized by the warlords, and what wasn't given to the government was kept for their own use. Tons of aid packages were showing up in neighboring countries where they were being sold for hard cash.

The UN was going through its usual torturous process of arguing like a bunch of third graders. The US, UK and France wanted the immediate deployment of UN Peacekeepers to stem the wholesale murders, but as usual, Russia and China didn't agree with anything the western members of the Permanent Security Council wanted.

Because they couldn't agree, the discussion was being taken to the General Assembly. In other words, the five third graders couldn't agree, so it was going to be left to a room full of kindergarteners to talk it to death before a vote could even be taken. While they fucked around in the comfort of New York City, hundreds of thousands of people would die.

It's probably good I'm not President because there would have already been about a hundred thousand US boots on the ground, kicking ass and putting a stop to things. I don't like bullies much, and don't think they deserve one ounce of leniency or forgiveness. I had a very close friend in high school that had been bullied relentlessly. Somehow, he managed to hide it from me, but I knew something was wrong. He wouldn't tell me what was happening.

Josh and I had grown up together, meeting on our first day of kindergarten. We'd become fast friends, and so had our parents. He'd always been a happy person, and a good friend. Our sophomore year of high school, things changed suddenly. He became withdrawn and no longer wanted to do any of the things we had always done together. We drifted apart until our contact was only when we'd pass each other in the hall at school.

This went on for almost a year until one night, at exactly 3:11 in the morning, my mother woke me up with the news that Josh had killed himself. He'd left a rambling note, trying to explain why taking his own life was preferable to asking for help. I never saw the note, but I got details from his big sister after the funeral.

Josh was gay. He'd hidden it from everyone as being gay at that time in a small, west Texas town wasn't something conducive to your health. He'd made a mistake and let something slip in front of some girls at school. They had apparently put two and two together and told their boyfriends who had tortured him mercilessly. He didn't name the boys in the note, or if he did his sister lied to me. Either way, it's probably for the best because I would have killed them if I had known who had pushed him to the point that slashing his wrists open seemed like the only option. No, I don't much care for bullies.

So with the news coming out of the region, and the influence of the first lady, POTUS had decided to send in a small force to corral the warlords. Short of declaring war on the country, there wasn't much he could do that hadn't already been done about the men in power, but he'd handed us a hunting license.

And then there was Doc and the rumors of Chinese agents in the area seeking viral samples. Neither Doc nor Delker would, or could, provide any more detail on what that was all about. We were just supposed to keep an eye and ear out for an opportunity to intercept one of the *agents* so Doc could get a look at what they were so interested in. Shutting down the warlords was the priority.

"Fifteen minutes!" The loadmaster bellowed, snapping me back to the moment.

Standing, I made the rounds, careful not to tangle my O2 line. I checked on each of my team, made them show me their altimeters, gave Doc a nod and a wink and stopped in front of Delker. He had changed into jungle camo and was giving his weapons a final inspection.

"You remember how to do this?"

I couldn't resist the temptation to tweak the asshole just a little. He shot me the bird and placed his hand on his rifle. I wish I knew what I'd done to this guy.

"Ten minutes!"

Hunter's Rain

The loadmaster came through the area, stopping to triple check the large pallet that would be going out the back door ahead of us. It contained a, well the technical term is shitload, of ammunition. There were also spare weapons, food, medical supplies and two changes of clothing for each of us. We didn't know how long we were going to be in-country, but we were coming prepared.

An additional pallet was for the Aussie SASR team that was already on the ground. Resupply of everything. They were meeting us at the LZ, and the contents of the two pallets would be spread across everyone's packs and humped fifteen miles up into the mountains where they had established a camp.

"Five minutes!"

I made a final walk around, happy with what I saw. Everyone was ready and relaxed. Well, Doc was ready, but I wasn't taking bets on relaxed. Nitro, however, was so relaxed he'd fallen back asleep. I kicked the bottom of his foot, and he opened his eyes and looked at me with a grin. Shaking my head, I moved back around out of the way and did a final radio check, ensuring we were all able to communicate with each other.

"Three minutes!"

We disconnected from the aircraft's O2 supply and began breathing from the small bottles secured to our bodies.

"Depressurizing," the pilot said over a couple of loudspeakers attached to the ceiling.

My ears popped, twice, then the loadmaster lowered the rear door. The warm atmosphere inside the plane was sucked out in an instant, replaced by air cold enough to make you keep the brass monkeys inside. Above the open door, a red light glowed into existence. There was a green one right beneath it and when it came on it would be time for us to go.

The pallets were equipped with an automatic release device that would deploy their chutes at two thousand feet. I personally don't like anything other than me having control over the deployment of my canopy and opted to not use one, even for backup. But that was my personal preference. Spider always had one, as did Nitro. To each their own. Maybe I am a control freak.

"Thirty seconds!" The loadmaster shouted over the rush of the wind past the open ramp. He was standing next to the first pallet, preparing to release it and give it a shove down the track and out the back of the aircraft. I started counting in my head when he yelled.

At twenty-five seconds he kicked the brake release and pushed the pallet. It began moving, slowly at first, but quickly picked up speed and rolled off the open ramp and disappeared.

"Ten seconds!" He called out, pushing the second pallet.

As it approached the ramp, I moved into the center of the cargo area and followed it, stopping six feet from the six-mile drop to the ground. A quick glance to check on my team, which was stacked up behind me and ready, and I focused my attention on the red light over the door.

I was still counting in my head and when I got to "two" I leaned forward onto the balls of my feet.

"GO, GO, GO!" The loadmaster shouted at the same time as the red light went dark and the green one began glowing.

9

Exiting an aircraft at night, at over thirty thousand feet, is a unique experience. It's easy to get disoriented, especially when the ground beneath you is dark. You just have to remember your training and not get caught up in the view, which can be breathtaking. But there wasn't that much to see. The Earth below was mostly dark with only a few scattered locations showing anything more than what seemed to be camp or cooking fires.

Far to the south, a large city gleamed like a diamond on black velvet, another one far to the northeast. They were a long way from where we were coming down, only visible because we were so high in the air. It wasn't long before I lost sight of them.

I did a quick check over the radio, getting a response from everyone, including a really nasty sounding belch from Spider. Since I was first off the ramp, I was the lowest, and the rest of the team had formed up on me. I was falling in a horizontal position, using the greater drag caused by my flattened body to control my speed.

Below, and slightly ahead, I could see the IR (Infrared) strobes flashing on the two pallets with my night vision goggles. Both were tumbling as they fell and I made an adjustment to continue following them so we'd come down close to where they landed.

"Look at your three," Two Step called over the radio, and I turned my head to see over my right shoulder.

Against the black backdrop, the muzzle flashes of a large firefight stood out clearly. It appeared to be several miles away. As I watched, it intensified for a few moments then died away to only an occasional flash. The victors mopping up the losers, most likely.

We were now under ten thousand feet, and I turned all of my attention back to the jump. I checked my altimeter, then verified the location of the tumbling pallets. They were a few hundred yards to my front and a couple of thousand feet below me.

The chutes on each pallet deployed just like they were supposed to, stabilizing their fall through the air. I steered slightly to my right to make sure there was plenty of space between them and us. If you're planning to open lower than the cargo, and not paying attention, you could potentially touchdown and a few moments later have a several hundred pound block land on top of your head. Not that I've ever heard of it actually happening, but I didn't want to become the example of what not to do in a training exercise.

We pulled at a thousand feet, everyone's canopy opening properly. At five hundred feet, I released my pack to drop below me and hang from a long tether. It would hit first, its weight not having to be absorbed by my legs when I touched down. From there we were on the ground quickly.

"Reaper one, good," I mumbled into the secure radio to confirm to the group that I was on the ground and hadn't sustained any injuries.

Quickly, in order, the rest of the team checked in. Poon confirmed Doc was down and Nitro reported on Delker. I hadn't issued either of them a radio, though there were spares squirreled away in Two Step's pack. I didn't want Doc on the comm net, potentially interrupting a transmission from someone that was critically important. And since I didn't trust Delker, I sure didn't want him able to listen in on our conversations in case we needed to relay something related to him or his assets.

We were in an open field, close to the edge of a tree line. The two pallets had come down a few hundred yards away, and I could see their IR strobes blinking patiently. The team immediately spread out into a defensive perimeter, going flat on the ground as all of us scanned the area for any threats. Doc was next to Poon and Delker had taken up a position as far from me as he could get.

"Nitro, see if our friends are in radio range," I mumbled over the radio after several minutes of not seeing anyone.

Nitro was our radio guy and, while the rest of us gathered up our canopies and stripped off the long underwear, he began transmitting a coded signal on a pre-arranged frequency.

"Forty-five mikes," he said over the encrypted comm channel.

"Copy," I said.

We gave him a minute to take off his insulation, then headed for the pallets. They had landed within fifty yards of each other, and the first order of business was to shut off the IR strobes. They weren't visible to the naked eye, but anyone who happened by and was wearing night vision would see them.

With Spider and Two Step on watch, the rest of us broke into them and began unloading the supplies for transfer to packs on our backs. The pallets were actually three by three by three-foot cubes made of thick, gray plastic. They were designed to be broken down easily once empty. While I disassembled them, Nitro, Poon and Doc set to work digging a shallow hole.

First, they removed a layer of the thick grass that grew in the field and set it aside, then tackled the rich soil with shovels that had been clipped to the inside of the pallets. It didn't take them long to dig down a couple of feet, and I dumped the pallet panels and their canopies into the hole. They quickly filled it in and put the turf they'd set aside on top to disguise the freshly turned earth. The extra dirt was scattered around the area.

While we had worked, Delker stood a few yards away typing on a satellite phone. Probably checking in with Langley, but I haven't survived this long by assuming someone I don't trust isn't doing something they shouldn't be doing. Coming up behind him quietly, I got a look over his shoulder before he knew I was there. Whoever he was communicating with, it was in a language I didn't recognize.

"Who are you talking to?" I asked right next to his ear.

He jumped and whirled to face me, backing up and lowering the phone.

"What the fuck do you think you're doing?" He hissed.

"Making sure you aren't playing games," I said. "Who are you talking to?"

Hunter's Rain

Nitro and Poon had been watching, and they drifted towards us as I took a step closer to Delker. Their movements didn't escape him, and he turned to keep them in sight.

"One of my local assets," he finally said with a snarl. "That's why I'm here. Remember?"

I held his eyes with mine for several long heartbeats, trying to decide if I believed him or not. Finally reconciling myself to the fact that I had to trust him for the moment, I nodded and walked away. We had about half an hour before the Aussies were due to arrive and I pulled out my own sat phone and sent a coded message to Fort Bragg, letting them know we were on the ground and awaiting the SASR to arrive at the LZ.

With nothing to do until the Aussies showed up, we spread out in a defensive posture. Poon took Doc with him and found a low hill fifty yards away to occupy. He set up on top, prone on his stomach with the fifty-caliber sniper rifle focused on the tree line, which was about three hundred yards away. With night vision and thermal optics, he would be able to see better than if the sun was up. With the suppressed rifle, he'd be able to vaporize just about any target he decided was a threat to the team.

The rest of us formed a circle around the area, prone in the tall grass of the field, watching and waiting. About fifteen minutes later there was a rustling to my left, and I looked over to see Nitro jerk back and slash at the ground with his knife.

"Nitro, sitrep," I mumbled into the radio, not overly concerned at the moment.

"Snake," he replied simply, then disappeared when he resumed his prone position in the grass.

"Was it big and black?" I recognized Spider's voice in my earpiece.

"That's a myth, mano. For truly big, you gotta go brown," Nitro shot back.

"Knock it off and stay focused," I transmitted quickly before they got out of hand.

A year ago I would have been more than happy to play along, but it's a different world when you're the one in charge of the lunatic asylum. The radio went quiet, and everyone settled down as we waited. The night was cool, for which I was thankful. We may have been in Africa, but the whole region we'd be operating in was at least three thousand feet above sea level and much cooler than the dense, steaming jungles nearer the coast. It would get cooler as we moved into the mountains, but cool is relative. It wouldn't be cold by any means.

Hunter's Rain

Lying there in the tall grass, I thought about Katie and wondered what she was doing. Thinking of her reminded me that I'd forgotten to take care of something before leaving Fort Bragg. I hadn't officially notified the Army that I had gotten married. She was now eligible to receive benefits if I didn't make it back, but I didn't know how much red tape she'd have to go through if something happened to me.

I'd been too busy planning the mission. Making sure we were ready and taking everything we needed. Double-checking to ensure everyone had received the proper vaccinations for the part of the world we were headed to. Doc, working for USAMRIID, was inoculated against just about everything for which a vaccine existed. The rest of us were good, but I was still glad I'd verified.

The mosquitoes had found us and were quickly growing in numbers when Poon alerted us that he had five targets moving in the trees. He gave a bearing, and after a few moments I was able to spot them through my night vision. The vegetation was dense, and I could see human forms with rifles, but no other details.

"Aussies are here," Nitro said over our comm channel a moment later.

"Show them a light," I said, telling him to flash an IR light a couple of times so they could spot our location.

I couldn't see his light, but a few seconds later there were three answering flashes from the trees. As the SASR moved into the open, I stood to greet them. They approached across the field, spreading out with their rifles up as they kept watch on the trees behind them. My friend, Staff Sergeant Lucas Martin, led the way, walking straight to me and giving me a hug.

"Good to see you, mate," he said, his teeth flashing white against the dark camo makeup covering his face.

"You're late," I said, smiling.

"Had a little dustup on the way," he shrugged.

I wondered if the firefight I'd seen while in free-fall had been them. It didn't matter, so I didn't bother asking.

My team had already distributed the supplies, and ours was loaded into our packs, ready to go. Five neat piles were waiting for the SASR, and they quickly loaded their packs and got ready to move.

Hunter's Rain

"Thanks for the goodies," Lucas said, hoisting his now heavy pack onto his shoulder and working it onto his back. "We were getting a bit low on the necessities."

We rallied our two teams and issued movement orders. Introductions could wait until we reached their camp. What mattered right now was getting there without drawing any attention to ourselves.

10

Their camp was well concealed amongst a thick stand of trees on the side of a mountain that disappeared into the clouds. It was daylight by the time we arrived, but little light made it through the canopy of heavily leafed trees far above our heads. It was humid as hell, mist hanging in the air, water dripping off of every branch and twig.

We hadn't been in camp more than a few minutes when an unearthly, snorting roar echoed through the forest. Another answered it before it died away. The Aussies didn't even look up, but all of us new arrivals looked around with our rifles up.

"What the fuck was that?" I asked Lucas, a little irritated at the grin on his face.

"Gorilla," he said.

"You're fucking with me," I stared at him.

"No, I'm really not. Scared the shit out of us when we first got here. Had no idea what it was. Tracked them and found a big family a couple of miles away. At least twenty of them. They're mellow and mind their own business. We don't mess with them, and they don't mess with us."

I shook my head, looking all around when the cry sounded again. Lucas laughed and motioned me to a small cooking fire one of his men had started as soon as we walked in. Water was heating in a battered pot, and I suspected he was going to offer me tea. Once we settled down on some rocks, he did just that. I accepted and looked around to check on my team while he busied himself with the preparations.

My guys were already trading barbs with the SASR, and I was glad to see that everything was good-natured. With a bunch of alpha males from two different countries, you never know what someone is going to say that will start a free for all. So far, everyone seemed to be on their best behavior. Tents were being erected and supplies removed from packs and stored.

It wasn't normal for us to be setting up a camp. We were almost exclusively of the drop in, ruin a bunch of bad guys' day, then go home, school. Setting up a semi-temporary operating base, replete with tents and a cache of supplies, was new for me. But it was what the mission called for, so here we were. Playing house with a bunch of Australians, and they weren't even the bikini wearing, bouncy blondes from Bondi Beach that I pictured whenever I thought of that country.

Lucas and I caught up as we sipped our tea. Nothing much had changed for either of us, other than my wedding, since the last time we spoke. He congratulated me and had to hear all about Katie.

When I was out of stories, he confessed he'd met a Kiwi (New Zealand) girl and was thinking about taking the plunge. Maybe. If he was ever home long enough to give it some serious thought.

"I've read the sitreps that were shared with us," I said, changing the topic to work before I started missing Katie too much. "What do I really need to know?"

"Aye, they probably sanitized those before sending them on," he grinned and drained his cup. "This is a bloody nasty corner of the world. Two tribes account for about ninety-nine percent of the population, and they've hated each other for so many generations that no one even knows why. It just is.

"The one in power has decided it's time to do something about the other one, and it's become open season. Warlords aligned with the central government are making everyone miserable that's from the wrong tribe. It's like… well, I'm not sure how to say this…"

He paused and looked down into his cup, then back up at me. His eyes slid across Spider and Delker, who had joined us.

"These people have no fucking regard for human life," he finally continued. "They come across an undesirable tribal member, and they'll kill them just for who they are. No hesitation. And not just kill. They love their AKs here, but they're also very fond of taking a machete to their enemies.

"We came across a village a couple of weeks ago. It had been devastated. Men, women, children; they were all dead. And not just dead. Most had been hacked to pieces. The women, even young girls, had been raped and shot in the back of the head when they were done. We counted two hundred and seven bodies.

"But that's not the worst. The houses, well not really houses, more like grass shacks. Anyway, they were all burned. In several of them, we found the skeletons of babies. Eleven babies. None of them any bigger than this."

He held his hands out in front of him, less than three feet apart.

"We tried to track the men that did it, but it was raining like hell, and we found it a few days after the massacre. Couldn't find them. Wanted to kill every one of them. Slow and painful."

We all sat there for a while. Quiet. Contemplative.

"What do you know about the warlords?" I finally asked, breaking the heavy silence.

"Not much," Lucas answered. "We were dropped in here without much intel and no local support. We've just been going out each night and hunting the raiding parties. We've made a dent and are starting to get noticed, but the locals are terrified to talk to us. No luck developing any assets."

"It takes a long time," Delker spoke up. "That's why we're here. I've got some assets that will feed us intel so we can start putting some of these fuckers in the ground."

OK, maybe the guy wasn't all bad. I fished through my pack and pulled out a plastic covered map and unfolded it.

"Show us where the village was. Maybe his asset will know which warlord is responsible. One of the guys that was involved probably talked. Bragged in a bar or a whorehouse. Someone will know something," I said.

Lucas nodded and took the map, looking at it closely for nearly a minute before he touched a spot a few miles north of our current location. Delker peered closely, noted the latitude and longitude marks and excused himself.

"While we're waiting on him, why are you going out at night? Seems like these guys are pretty bold and wouldn't be worried about attacking during the day."

Hunter's Rain

"It's not that," Lucas said. "They want everyone in one convenient location when they raid a village. In the daytime, people are off hunting, fishing, working if they have a job, farming, doing whatever it is they do to survive. The kids will be off playing or with one of their parents. Too scattered. But if they attack at night, then everyone is home, and they get the most bang for their buck."

I nodded in agreement with his explanation. Sitting there in the misty morning light I wanted to go throw up. This is the kind of shit that goes on in the world that could be stopped if we really wanted to. There's no hand-wringing and interminable political debate needed. No time to waste while the media conducts public opinion polls. None of the, "it's not our country so it's not our problem" bullshit. The last time I checked, we're supposedly all of the same species.

Powerless innocents are being slaughtered, and we have the ability to put thousands of well trained and heavily armed Soldiers and Marines on the ground to stop it. But let's allow it to continue while we publicly condemn the country where it's happening and impose economic sanctions. I'm sure that will work. After all, it's been so effective in the past.

11

It was dark and raining when we set out from camp that night. In fact, it had been raining since late afternoon when a tremendous thunderstorm had passed directly overhead and blasted everyone awake with a crack of thunder that sounded like God had reached down and clapped his hands right above us.

"Excuse me," Spider had called out from the tent he was sharing with Two Step before the rumbling echoes had subsided. There were snorts of laughter, then everyone that wasn't on watch rolled over and went back to sleep.

Now we were moving along a narrow game trail that was nothing more than a track of slippery mud cutting through the vegetation. One of Lucas's men was on point, a slim marathon runner looking guy with long blonde hair and an impressive mustache. I thought he looked like a really skinny Hulk Hogan. I was ten yards behind him at the head of the rest of the joint team, Lucas bringing up the rear of the main body. Nitro was ten yards farther back, bringing up the rear.

Delker had managed to contact one of his assets after our conversation and had gotten a call back sometime in the afternoon. According to him, we were looking for a warlord named Ngabo. One of the Aussies spoke the local dialect and said the name meant, "Soldier". Personally, I was offended and would take great pleasure in introducing him to a real soldier. A grainy photo of Ngabo had been texted to Delker's sat phone and I made sure everyone took a good look at it.

He operated out of a small village that was twelve miles from our camp. About forty men counted themselves as his army, but in reality were nothing more than a bunch of assholes that'd picked up a gun and a machete. The population of the village was just over one hundred, and word was that he treated them like his own personal slaves.

This was the enigma of this part of Africa. The village was populated with members of the same tribe as those in power. The same tribe as Ngoba. Yet he had zero compunctions about taking over their town. I hoped that the villagers wouldn't rise up in his defense. I couldn't imagine that happening, but this was a seriously fucked up place.

We had originally planned to set up an ambush for the warlord and his followers, taking them out as they headed into the jungle for their next nocturnal raid, but the asset had relayed that they were staying put tonight to celebrate. Their celebration was the capture of fourteen young schoolgirls that were going to be the center of attention for the evening.

Dirk Patton

I would have preferred to either encounter the men out in the jungle or arrive well after midnight and take them as they slept off whatever local brew they were drinking. But when Lucas and I had heard about the girls, we'd decided to try to get there early enough to crash the party before it kicked into high gear.

This was more dangerous and not the best tactical decision by either of us, but it was the right thing to do. The girls supposedly ranged in age from eleven to fifteen, and it had taken us all of half a second to make the call. Besides, both of our teams were spoiling for a fight. Especially the Aussies, who were looking to exorcise some demons.

As we'd prepared to head out, Nitro had worked with the SASR comm specialist and gotten all of us on the same frequency. I'd reluctantly issued a radio to Delker and Doc, cautioning both of them to stay off the air unless there were something urgent they needed to communicate. They'd agreed, Doc readily, but Delker had shot me a dirty look. Fuck him. He didn't have to like it, he just had to do it.

We arrived at the outskirts of the village two hours after dark. The rain had stopped, but the humidity was so high I was starting to feel a little like Aquaman. I couldn't take a breath of air that wasn't saturated with water. The ground was spongy, and my boots made a slight sucking noise every time I lifted a foot to take a step. Poon, with Doc and Delker in tow, broke off from the group and headed for a high point that overlooked the village. The Aussies didn't have a sniper with them and were very glad to have my guy watching over us.

I had rank on Lucas but had still talked to him privately before assuming operational command of our merged units. It's called courtesy and respect. He'd had no issue, or if he did he hid it well. Now, I twirled my finger in the air, and everyone spread out.

We'd had an operational briefing before leaving camp, and each man knew what his job and area of responsibility was. Nitro had brought along a small laptop that had a satellite modem, and once we knew where the village was he'd downloaded a recent real-time image. All of us had huddled around the small screen to get a look, and I'd made assignments.

We didn't have to talk to get into position, just moved through the thick foliage like ghosts in the night. In less than five minutes I had received confirmation from each of them that they were in place and ready to go.

"Poon. Talk to me," I mumbled into the radio as I peered at the small collection of mud and grass huts through my night vision.

"Seventeen, one – seven, buildings. Eight vehicles. Three with pintle-mounted machine guns. Two guards at the east end, one to the west. One guard at a building in the center. None of the other structures are guarded. Got four locations showing light, and I can hear music and voices, but no movement other than the guards."

Poon had a bird's eye view from a location he'd spotted on the satellite image. I checked with Spider, Lucas and Two Step, who were each at strategic surveillance points, but they didn't see anything that Poon hadn't already reported. At a command from me, all of us tightened the perimeter we'd formed around the village so everyone had eyes on our targets.

I quickly designated each lit building as one through four, issuing breaching assignments. Once they were cleared, we'd move on to the rest of the village. All of the residents would be herded out onto the mud track that was the only road through town. Once they were there, we'd make sure there weren't any of the bad guys hiding amongst them. When we were satisfied that all of the warlord's troops had been ferreted out and dealt with, we'd leave the villagers in peace.

Hunter's Rain

"Poon. On my order," I mumbled.

Receiving his acknowledgment in my earpiece, I quickly checked with the rest of the team to make sure nothing had changed in the village.

"Engage," I said.

He was far enough away that I couldn't hear the report of his suppressed sniper rifle, but I could see the results. One of the eastern guard's head exploded, and before his buddy could do anything other than stare at the body with his mouth hanging open, he died too. Moments later the western guard went down, then a heartbeat later the one in front of the dark building.

"All targets neutralized," Poon radioed as the last one dropped to the mud. "No others in sight."

"GO, GO, GO!" I said over the radio.

We flowed out of the dark jungle and dashed across the open space leading up to the huts showing light. Loud, alcohol-fueled voices were clear in the humid air as I pressed my back against the wall next to the door of hut number one. Well, not really a door. Just an opening in the wall with a ratty blanket hung for privacy.

Dirk Patton

Spider and Nitro were at my back, ready to follow me through. At hut number two, Lucas had two of his team members stacked behind him. Two Step and the remaining Aussies were keeping an eye on the rest of the village, making sure the residents didn't come running when the fireworks started. Poon stayed where he was, keeping an eagle eye on the entire area, and would suppress anyone who came out of huts three or four.

Delker had wanted to be a part of the assault, but I had flatly refused. He'd argued that he was a SEAL, and I'd told him I didn't give a fuck. He hadn't worked or trained as an operator for years and had never trained with my team. We didn't need another body badly enough to run the risk. I think I actually hurt his feelings, but I didn't care. This wasn't about anyone's ego. He was cooling his heels with Poon and Doc.

I would have preferred to just toss a couple of fragmentation grenades through each doorway, let them wreak their havoc, then go in and clean up any survivors. But we didn't know where the girls were, so couldn't take the chance. We'd just have to rely on surprise and violence of action to give us an advantage. Well, that, plus we were sober and it sounded like there wasn't anyone in the huts that wasn't already deep in the booze.

A glance over my shoulder to check on Spider and Nitro. Spider was right behind me and gave a barely perceptible nod to indicate he was ready. No jokes, no funny faces, nothing that wasn't intense focus on the job at hand. He was a professional and had put his war face on, just like I knew he would when it was go time.

I looked across at Lucas, raising my hand to start a silent count so we could coordinate the beginning of the assault. Before I could even extend my fingers to initiate the timing, the curtain covering the door right next to me was suddenly pulled aside. A man, more a boy really as he couldn't have been much older than eighteen, stepped out.

He was barefoot, wearing ragged pants and a faded yellow tank top. An ancient AK-47 was slung around his bony shoulders, a machete swinging from his belt. It was light inside the hut and very dark outside, and he couldn't see us. I let him take a step forward until the curtain fell back in place.

Using the same hand I'd been preparing to count with, I clamped his throat with enough force to prevent a shout, or any breath coming in our out of his lungs. With my other, I grabbed the rifle, covering the trigger guard with my palm so he couldn't work a finger in and squeeze off a shot.

His eyes went wide, the whites abnormally large from fear as I spun him towards Spider. We had worked together long enough that we didn't need to communicate. He'd seen the threat, saw what I was doing, and was ready as I twisted the man's body towards him. Ka-Bar knife in hand, he thrust deeply, and I felt the body go rigid from the shock of the injury.

I held the man away from me as Spider withdrew the blade and stabbed through his rib cage, piercing his heart. He went limp, and I released the corpse as Nitro took the dead weight and moved it around the corner into deeper shadows. It only took him a few seconds, then he was back in the stack.

Lucas nodded when I signed, and I started the count. Three... Two... One... GO!

12

I rolled my body around the corner of the opening and pushed through the filthy curtain. My rifle was up, the muzzle the first thing to enter the room. Spider's hand was hard on my left shoulder until I rolled to the right and he released me to move left. Nitro was tight behind him and would come straight in.

The hut was nothing more than a large room with a dirt floor. Half a dozen oil lamps were scattered around the space, providing plenty of light. The electronics in my night vision automatically shut down, and I could clearly see everything and everyone in the building.

Eleven men were scattered across the floor, some seated on blankets, others on the dirt. All were drinking and shouting encouragement to the man in the back who was naked and standing over a small nude form that was huddled against the wall. His penis was erect as he forced a small girl's legs apart.

I saw and registered all of this in less than a second. All of the men were intent on the show, and none had noticed us yet. Time to change that.

My rifle was tight to my shoulder, and I adjusted slightly to put the sights on target and shot the naked man in the head. He dropped instantly, falling on top of the cowering girl, eliciting a scream from her. There was a shout from his audience when he fell, some of them thinking the show was starting, but others realized what had happened and scrambled for their weapons.

I began firing single, methodical shots from my suppressed rifle. Behind me I could hear two more rifles firing, then there were no more targets. Twelve men dead in less than eight seconds with hardly any sound. Perhaps we would have had a fight if they all hadn't been drunk and focused on watching the rape of a young girl, but we didn't. It was a slaughter.

"Check her," I hissed to Spider as he and Nitro were making sure none of the bad guys were playing opossum. We didn't need an asshole to pop up and start shooting when our backs were turned.

I moved to the door and twitched the curtains aside, listening intently but not hearing any sounds of disturbance from the hut Lucas had gone in. Nitro kept checking bodies by stabbing his eight-inch Ka-Bar into the most convenient vital spot. Spider hauled the dead rapist off the girl and tossed his corpse onto the dirt floor without a second thought.

She was completely nude, and I couldn't tell from her face, but from the development of her body I didn't think she was any older than thirteen. Spider reached for her arm, but she shrank away in fear, opening her mouth to cry or scream. He didn't know which, but what mattered was that she remain quiet. Clamping a hand over her mouth, he held a finger to his lips. She nodded after a few moments and he released her, tumbled a body off a blanket and wrapped it around her shoulders like a cloak. He got her on her feet and moving towards the door.

"Building one, clear," I mumbled into my radio.

"Two clear."

I recognized Lucas's voice several seconds later.

"Coming out," I said and signed for Spider and Nitro to form up on me. We still had more work to do.

Outside, Spider led the girl to the middle of the mud track that cut through the area. He had her sit down and signed for one of the Aussies that was keeping watch on the village to come over and guard her. We were sure she was a captive we'd just rescued and posed no threat, but you don't take chances and leave someone unguarded.

Lucas and his team exited the second hut moments later, exchanging nods with us before moving to the next two shacks that were showing light. We had already planned this before beginning the assault, and I led my team to the largest, number four, while he went to number three. When both teams were stacked, I started the count.

Hut four was the largest structure in the village, boasting two rooms. As I pushed through, a guard seated in a rickety chair looked up, eyes going wide when he recognized the danger. He reached for his rifle, which was leaned against the mud and straw wall next to him. I shot him twice in the chest and stepped past as the body flopped to the ground.

Another man was sleeping on a filthy sheet, and I put a round in his head before he could wake up. Several more suppressed shots sounded then I heard Nitro mumble, "clear" from right behind me. We moved to the curtained doorway into the second room, Spider tight to my left. Nitro would watch our backs as we made entry.

I moved as soon as I felt Spider's grip on my shoulder. Shoving the fabric aside, I stepped through into a small room that was lit by a single candle on the floor in the far corner. Night vision remained active, and I could see a thick pad of blankets spread out to roughly the dimensions of a king sized bed. A tall, thin black man was asleep on his back in the middle, two young girls completely nude and huddled on either side of him.

It took half a second to sweep the room and tell that the three of them were the only occupants. A rifle was leaned in the corner, several feet from where the man slept. His clothes were in a pile next to it, but I didn't see any discarded clothing for the girls. They must have been stripped naked somewhere else before being brought in. Both were awake, staring at us in fear. But they didn't try to move, not even to cover their nudity.

"Let me," Spider mumbled quietly.

I nodded and kept my rifle at the ready as he stepped forward and moved the girl on the left off the bedding. He waved at the other, and she carefully scooted until she was against the wall, but too close to the rifle for my taste. I quickly circled around the sleeping mat and picked it up. Sure, she had no reason to want to grab it and shoot us. I knew that, but did she? After what she'd been through?

Spider stood over the man, peering closely at his face for several seconds before glancing at me and nodding. We had Ngabo. Drawing his pistol, Spider delivered a savage kick to his exposed balls.

Ngabo hissed in pain, snapping awake instantly and trying to sit up. But as his head came off the blanket, Spider stepped in and kneed him in the face. He fell back, moaning, one hand holding his bruised testicles, the other pressed to what was almost surely a broken nose.

Dropping a knee onto the man's stomach, Spider slapped the hand away from his face, shoved his pistol's suppressor against the soft skin under his jaw and pulled the trigger. Ngabo twitched once as the round went into his skull.

"Four clear," I mumbled into the radio.

Almost immediately, Lucas called back that three was clear as well. Spider stood, spat on the corpse, then helped the girl on his side of the room to her feet. We each picked up a piece of the bedding and covered their bare skin before leading them out to where the first one was being guarded.

We made entry in all of the remaining huts, finding only frightened villagers. Except for the hut that had been guarded. The rest of the young girls were huddled together in a back corner. All of them had been stripped naked, and we spent a few minutes collecting blankets so they could cover themselves.

As each hut was cleared, the occupants were herded at gunpoint into the center of the road. Maybe I should have felt bad, doing this to them. But, until I was certain we'd gotten every one of Ngabo's men, I didn't give a crap if we were scaring them or not.

Once every building was empty and had been thoroughly searched, I walked to where Delker, Lucas and one of his men were standing in front of the cowering villagers. All of the frightened people were on their knees, hands on top of their heads. No one had argued or tried to resist. They were too accustomed to being told what to do by the men with the guns.

"Thirty-six, plus Ngabo," I said to Delker. "Your guy said forty-one."

Delker nodded and brought out his sat phone. I watched him look for a number in the memory, then place a call. While he was doing this, Mad Max, the member of Lucas's team that spoke the local language, began talking with one of the villagers. The man he was speaking with appeared to be the oldest male, and I assumed he was the headman, or chief, or whatever title they used. He wrapped up his conversation before Delker got off the phone.

"That's the village chief," Max said, nodding at the man he'd been speaking with. "He says that all of the people we have are his and not Ngabo's."

"You trust him?" I asked.

He looked at Lucas, who nodded.

"I don't necessarily trust him, but I believe he's telling the truth about this," he answered.

"Ngabo and his army were working their way through the village women before they brought the girls in. The chief says thank you for killing the man who raped and murdered his daughter."

"Forty-one was an old count from several weeks ago," Delker interrupted. "No way to know what the current one was, and I doubt even Ngabo knew. From what I've heard, if one of his followers gave him any reason, he would have no hesitation in pulling the trigger on them."

I nodded and looked at Lucas.

"What about the girls?" He asked.

"The chief says the village will take them in. They can stay, or he'll help them get back to their families if he can," Mad Max said.

"Believe he's sincere? I don't want to leave them here to be massacred because they're the wrong tribe, or family, or whatever," I said.

"I believe he is," he answered. "And, they're all the same ancestral tribe. Ngabo was just a thug. This had nothing to do with anything other than him doing whatever he wanted."

13

We left the villagers, melting into the jungle and forming up to head back to camp. The game trail we were using paralleled the rough track for half a mile before turning and heading up the side of a mountain. We hadn't reached the turn when the Aussie on point signaled, and we all froze.

A couple of moments later we spread into the underbrush at a sign from him that there was someone approaching. Lucas and I silently made our way to where he had sought cover behind a thick tree. He was focused in the direction of the road and didn't turn his head when we knelt next to him.

"What?" Lucas mumbled.

"Engines approaching," he mumbled, pointing with the blade of his hand.

It was raining again, and I couldn't hear anything over the sound of water striking the leaves and ground, but I wasn't going to dismiss something just because someone else could hear it and I couldn't. A few moments later I began to pick up the sound of a motor straining to move its load on the muddy track.

"Headed for the village," Lucas said. "No one around here is going to have a vehicle unless they're a bad guy."

I nodded and issued commands over the radio for the team to move to the road. We pushed through the undergrowth and stopped at the abrupt forest edge where it had been carved out of the earth.

"How long?" I asked the point man.

"A minute, maybe." He answered.

I knew he was basing his answer on the arrival of the vehicle strictly on the sounds that were reaching his ears. Hopefully, he was conservative with his estimate. We split, sending half the team to the far side where they concealed themselves in the foliage. Two Step took a few seconds to scatter tire spikes as he crossed the track.

The spikes we carried were made of machined aluminum and were very strong and extremely sharp. For safe carry in our packs, they were encased inside a protective plastic sheath that peeled off easily. Flat on one side for stability, they had a small forest of three-inch spikes that protruded straight up from the ground.

They would sink slightly into the mud under the weight of a vehicle tire, but were designed to penetrate the rubber and steel belts rather than just be pushed deep below the surface. The first time I'd witnessed them being demonstrated was on a training range at Fort Bragg. Thick mud so deep it was damn near impossible to walk in had been the test environment.

They were tossed out by hand, the flat, weighted side landing face down so the razor sharp spikes were pointing at the sky. We'd driven several different vehicles across them at everything from a creeping five miles an hour to a mud blasting forty, and without fail, they'd flattened the tires on every attempt. I'd made the mistake of trying to pick one up by its spikes and had wound up with nearly thirty stitches in my hand.

We tested them on every surface we could think of. Asphalt, sand, the soft bottom of a stream, rocks, you name it and we tried it. Rocks in a dry stream bed were the only environment where the spikes didn't perform one hundred percent of the time, and that was because there were occasions when they would fall between two larger stones and the sharp points wouldn't be pointed directly up.

Spikes in place, we settled in to wait. Soon, headlights were visible in the distance, creating two bright halos in the mist filled air. The engine noise grew in volume, and I could hear a miss as at least one cylinder failed to fire on each stroke of the piston. That most likely ruled out a government vehicle, even in a third world shithole. As poor as they might be, they did find the money to keep their meager equipment running better than this.

As the vehicle continued to approach, it became apparent it was a truck of some sort. The lights were too high off the ground to be a car. It was moving slow, either because of the engine problems or the road conditions, and I could hear mud squishing under its tires.

Poon had climbed a few feet up into a large tree fifty yards back into the jungle and had a clear line of sight to the area of the road where the spikes waited. He was our backup just in case things went sideways. Doc and Delker were at the base of the tree, keeping an eye on his back and guarding the large pack he'd left on the ground.

After what seemed an eternity, the truck came into view. It was an ancient, four-wheel drive Toyota Hi-Lux, about as common in Africa as a Chevy or Ford is in America. The engine gasped, knocked and whined, but somehow kept the vehicle moving. Between the rain and headlights, I couldn't make out the occupants, but knew someone that could.

"Reaper five, what do you see?" I called to Poon over the radio.

Hunter's Rain

"Three in the cab, all with rifles," he answered immediately. "Two more in an open bed. There's a pintle, but no machine gun visible."

"Windows on the cab up or down?" I asked.

"Down," he answered a moment later.

"Copy," I said and issued a quick set of orders.

We weren't going to mess around and wind up in a firefight with these guys. I wanted to hit them hard and fast and be on our way. It's only in the movies that you give the bad guys a chance to fight back. Even the most untrained person can get off a lucky shot.

The right front tire of the truck ruptured with a loud bang when it encountered a spike. The engine quieted to a knocking idle as the driver took his foot off the gas. Within a very few feet, they rolled to a stop, the mud and flat tire quickly overcoming momentum. They were sitting ducks, and I didn't need to issue any commands to begin the attack.

Through my night vision, I watched as the head of one of the men in back exploded, his body flipping over the side into the mud. A moment later, the second one met the same fate. I hadn't heard a sound from Poon's suppressed rifle and the guys in front were too busy arguing to have noticed. Probably trying to decide who was going to get out and change the tire.

Spider dashed forward from the bushes next to me, Two Step right behind him. From the far side, I could see two of the Aussies running onto the road. Both groups approached the cab from slightly behind, out of view of the occupants. Spider and the SASR trooper each had a grenade in their hand, pulling the pins as they approached.

With their backup providing security, they stepped forward and each tossed their grenade through the open windows. They had already cooked off two to three seconds of the five-second fuse and as soon as the baseball sized explosive left their hands they spun away and moved to the rear of the truck. Two Step and the second Aussie backed away, their rifles up and trained on the cab, ready to open fire if a door opened or a rifle appeared.

Shouts of panic erupted from within the cab, then the two grenades detonated. The whole truck shook on its suspension, and the windshield and rear window shattered before being blown out by the force of the blasts. Now, Two Step and his counterpart on the opposite side of the vehicle took the lead and dashed forward, rifles up and ready to ensure the three men in the cab were dead.

Hunter's Rain

They checked, then stepped back and each fired a round into the shattered heads of the three occupants. There was little chance the men were still alive, but when you start leaving things to chance, they have a way of coming back to bite you in the ass.

"Clear," Two Step transmitted, and I gave the command to form up and get out of there.

Spider and Two Step took a few seconds to retrieve the tire spikes, returning them to their protective cases. Poon slithered down out of the tree and less than a minute after the grenades exploded we had disappeared into the jungle.

14

We arrived back at our camp at 0330. The rain had stopped, but every leaf was wet, and you couldn't move without getting doused with rainwater. Thick mist blanketed the jungle floor, and it was a little unnerving to not know what you were stepping on until you felt it under your foot. I knew there were a lot of very venomous snakes in this part of Africa, and hoped the weather had them holed up somewhere.

All of us were soaked to the skin, but when we got to camp the first order of business was to check our weapons. We each did a quick cleaning, then oiled the hell out of them. In dry, dusty parts of the world, it's important to go very easy on the amount of oil as it will quickly attract sand and jam up the works. But we were fighting nearly constant moisture and needed to make sure the moving parts didn't have a chance for any rust or corrosion to form.

Weapons taken care of, I moved into the confines of my tent and changed clothes, carefully drying my feet and applying a small amount of powder before pulling on dry socks. There are a whole host of problems that develop very quickly if your feet stay wet. Blisters, boils, loss of circulation, and several other conditions that I had no desire to experience. Spreading out my wet items, I hoped they'd dry, but with the high humidity I wasn't very optimistic.

Spider took care of getting watch assignments made while I composed a brief summary of our evening's activities on my sat phone. When it was complete, I entered the command to encrypt the message and called Nitro. He stuck his head in and took the blocky unit when I held it up. He would connect it to a piece of comm gear he carried that would download and compress the file before transmitting it to an orbiting satellite in a burst that would last no longer than a fraction of a second.

Housekeeping chores taken care of, I pulled on my boots, grabbed my rifle and went out to take a seat by the small fire. Lucas walked up and plopped down next to me while I prepared an MRE. Soon, everyone that wasn't on watch was gathered around. A couple of Lucas's team broke out some kind of meat they worked onto sticks and propped over the flames to cook. My guys immediately began trying to work out a trade of different parts of their MREs for some of the meat. They didn't even know what it was, and didn't care. Anything fresh and cooked is almost always better than freeze dried.

"What is that?" I asked Lucas in a low voice, nodding at the fire.

"Some kind of little tree dwelling rodent," he said. "Smyth trapped it last night with a snare. Bloody sick of MREs."

I grinned and happily stirred my tuna casserole.

"You guys run across that kind of shit before?" Spider asked the group in general.

"Aye, mate. We 'ave." The one Lucas had called Smyth spoke up as he turned the spits of roasting rat. I had to admit it didn't smell half bad. "Fucking wankers don't give a sod about anyone or anything. Just want people to be afraid of them and to get their peckers wet."

Spider sat staring into the fire, munching his food slowly.

"You don't sound like an Aussie, Sergeant," I said to Smyth.

"Thank you! Bloody glad I don't talk like a bunch of convict scum," he grinned, referring to Australia's past role as banishment for England's undesirable prisoners. "Liverpool. Had the misfortune of falling for a big tittied Aussie girl. Made the move and by the time I arrived she was already giving some poor South African bastard his jollies. By then, too late to go back and the weather is much better down under."

Hunter's Rain

Lucas reached out and took one of the spits of meat, slicing nearly half of it off with his knife before returning the stick to the fire.

"Here now, Lucas! That's bloody improper as hell!" Smyth protested.

"Just the descendent of convict scum acting the part, old boy."

Lucas perfectly mimed an upper-class British accent and smiled as he sank his teeth into the cooked rat.

"See wot I mean?" Smyth looked at me, grinned and pointed at Lucas.

"Know of anyone else we need to pay a visit?" I asked Lucas.

"Not at the moment. But there are a couple of villages a few klicks south of here that haven't been bothered yet. Thought it might be a good idea to patrol in their area and see if we can catch any of the bad guys up to no good," he said, wiping juice from the meat off his chin.

"Delker, anything from your end?" I asked the CIA man who was on the far side of the fire.

"It's the middle of the fucking night," he answered grudgingly. "I'll make some calls tomorrow."

Dirk Patton

I was going to have to press the issue with the prick. He was supposed to be here to support us. Provide intel about where our specific talents could do the most good. But it seemed as if he didn't want to offer up anything that I didn't have to drag out of him and wasn't in any hurry to try and obtain new information. Whatever his issue with me was, we needed to get it dealt with. Standing up I caught his eye, tilted my head and walked a few yards out into the jungle. A few moments later he joined me.

"What?" He said with an aggressive tone and stance.

"That's what I want to know," I said, forcing myself to remain calm and not wrap my hands around his throat. "You've obviously got a problem with me, and in my judgment it's affecting the mission. So, you want to talk to me about it or do I make a call and have your ass yanked out of here?"

"You couldn't make that happen," he sneered. "I'm the only one with assets in the region and you need me."

"Not as much as you think," I said, bluffing.

He was right about me needing the information his assets could provide, but I wasn't going to admit that to him and give him the upper hand.

"You're an asshole," he said. "You know that?"

"What have I missed?" I asked, genuinely curious. "I've never met you. What the hell is your problem?"

"You really don't know?" He asked. "Jesus, the bitch didn't tell you?"

"Who? Tell me what?" I asked, growing more than a little perturbed.

"Steve Johnson?" He asked like I was supposed to recognize the name.

"No clue."

I shook my head for emphasis.

"He's my brother."

"Whoopty fucking doo," I said. "I still don't know what the hell you're talking about."

"He was engaged to your wife until you swooped in and took her away. He got a little carried away and accessed your file and got his ass in a ringer, big time."

"Well then that's his fucking fault," I said, leaning forward. "I didn't do a goddamn thing to him."

"You stole his fiancée, asshole," he said. "You don't do that. Take another man's woman. And now his career's in the toilet because of you and that cunt."

I didn't even think about it, just threw the first punch. My fist caught him square in the face, knocking him flat on his ass. Stepping forward, I leaned in to grab him, but he knew the same tricks I did. He swept my legs out from under me and threw two punches as I hit the ground. Both connected and hurt like hell. Rolling, I snapped an elbow into his face and went with the momentum, coming down on top of him. He threw me and I came to my feet, moving in as he launched himself at me.

This wasn't a Hollywood stuntman fight. We weren't throwing punches like it was some barroom brawl in the old west, and weren't yelling and shouting. It was fast, hard and potentially lethal if either of us missed a block. I had split his nose open and had a cut over my left eye. He had my arm locked up and was going for a strike to my throat.

I blocked it and rocketed another elbow into the side of his face, breaking the hold on my arm. Spinning, I was reaching for his exposed neck when we were both tackled to the ground. Spider and Nitro pulled me away as Lucas and Smyth subdued Delker.

"Get the fuck off me!" I snarled, but Spider had the position and leverage to hold me and wasn't letting go.

"Can't kill a Company man, boss," he whispered in my ear.

I kept struggling until Nitro stepped directly behind and locked me up, lifting my feet off the ground and turning me away. I heard Spider telling Lucas to get Delker out of there. Several seconds later I stopped struggling against Nitro's grip and just stood there panting.

"You done?" Spider was in front of my face looking into my eyes. "We let you go, are you done?"

"Get your fucking hands off of me," I growled, struggling.

Nitro was strong as an ox and I couldn't break his embrace without causing some damage. Despite my enraged state, I wasn't going to hurt a friend and teammate.

"Not until you calm down and promise not to kill him. Or us," Spider said, leaning in and grinning at me.

After a few more seconds, I nodded agreement. Nitro released me and quickly stepped back. Adrenaline was surging through my body, and I was still pissed.

"What the fuck?" Spider asked, staying a safe distance away. "You were going to kill that guy. Don't you know it's bad juju to ice one of those fucks?"

My breathing was coming under control and I explained what had set me off. Spider listened, nodding as I talked. Nitro stayed behind me, presumably to stop me from turning and going after Delker.

"So the guy's a crusty semen stain," he said. "So what? Since when do you let douche bags like that get under your skin?"

"Since he's talking about my wife," I said, then realized I sounded like I was in high school. "I guess I should have settled for knocking him on his ass."

"Probably, boss," Nitro said from behind me. "Wanna bet he's already on the phone complaining about you? Gonna be a shit storm when we get home."

"Like I give a fuck," I said.

Spider grinned and nodded, knowing I didn't care if the CIA complained about me.

"Let's just stay away from him and get some sleep," Spider said after a few moments.

I nodded but knew I was too keyed up to sleep. The adrenaline was burning off, and the bloodlust had subsided, but I wasn't anywhere near ready to sleep.

"I've got first watch," I said. "You go get some sleep."

"OK." He looked at my face for several long seconds. "But don't shoot that miserable fuck while we're sleeping."

I smirked at him and led the way back into camp.

15

It was midafternoon, and I was sitting in front of the small fire after having gotten several hours of sleep. I was sharing an MRE with Lucas, discussing the upcoming patrol we were going to conduct near the villages he had mentioned. It wasn't raining, and the mist had lifted, leaving cloying humidity and a baking sun. Steam rose from the saturated ground, and it was miserably hot.

"Can I talk to you?"

I looked up to see Delker standing on the far side of the fire. Lucas glanced at me, and I nodded that everything was cool. Spider was watching from the flap in his tent, but I ignored him. There wouldn't be any more fighting. I'd lost my head the night before, and it wouldn't happen again.

"Talk," I said, meeting his eyes and noting the crooked nose and swelling on his face.

"I wanted to apologize," he said, lowering his gaze to the flames. "I was out of line."

I couldn't have been more surprised if he'd walked up and told me an alien spaceship had just landed and was full of Victoria's Secret models, asking for me by name. Staring back at him, I tried to determine if he was sincere, or if this was some game he was playing. I'm a fairly good judge of character, but you don't become a field officer in the CIA if you're not an accomplished liar. Still, I didn't see anything other than genuine regret.

"Yes, you were," I said, without any hostility. "Until last night I didn't know that Katie was engaged when I met her. Shit happens. If your brother stepped on his dick because he couldn't handle losing her, that's his fault. She made a choice, and it wasn't him."

He nodded and just stood there. Either unsure of what to say, or had nothing else to offer and didn't know how to walk away.

"So, your name is Johnson?" Lucas asked.

"I've got ID that says it's Delker."

Lucas and I both snorted at that one. I made a mental note to find out what names Katie used when she was in the field. Just in case I ever needed to find her.

After Delker had squirmed for almost a minute, I decided to let him off the hook. I didn't like him, and we'd never be friends, but I still needed him on this operation.

"Any word from your assets?" I asked, then noticed Spider was still watching and so was Nitro.

"Relax ladies," I raised my voice so they could hear me. "We aren't going to kill each other this afternoon."

Nitro shook his head, walked over to Spider and handed him what looked like a twenty-dollar bill. Assholes.

"There's three warlords active in the area we're going into tonight. Each claims the territory, and they've had the occasional skirmish, but so far none of them has come out on top. One of them is making a move tonight. The two strongest ones are going to be fighting each other, and the third is planning to sit back to see who comes out on top.

"I was thinking that while two of them are duking it out, we pay the third one a visit and take him off the playing field. The other two will suffer heavy losses, and the winner will be ripe for us to take out. Three of them off the board in twenty-four hours."

Delker stood there looking at me after he finished speaking. I had to grudgingly give the man some credit. He had been an ass hat. He knew he'd been an ass hat, and now he was trying to make up for it. I briefly considered that he might be up to something, but dismissed the thought.

"Not a bad idea," Lucas chimed in after several seconds of silence. I finally nodded and had Delker sit down and show us on the map.

Hunter's Rain

We talked and planned for the rest of the afternoon. Assignments were made based on the information we had, but everyone had been in the game long enough to know things would get adjusted on the fly. That's just the nature of combat.

As evening approached, we began preparing to move. Weapons were checked and double checked. Extra magazines were loaded. Gear was gone over and donned. Knives were sharpened, and Nitro got into an impromptu throwing contest with Smyth.

Their target was a thick tree covered in vines, and the whole thing started when Spider noticed large spiders moving up and down the trunk. He has his handle for a reason, having an unreasonable fear of the little creatures. Granted, I'm not fond of them either, but I don't act like a pre-teen girl when I see one.

I didn't know what kind of spiders these were, but they had large, hairy bodies about the size of a silver dollar and long, red legs. When Spider noticed them, he jumped off the log where he was sitting. In a near panic, he checked himself to make sure none of them were crawling on him.

His reaction caught Nitro's attention, who, with a chuckle, flicked a small blade so fast it was a blur. It speared the body of one of the insects and neatly pinned it to the tree. A moment later, a thin knife thrown by Smyth impaled another. Spider stood there grinning, watching as the two men took turns. Neither missed, both eventually running out of knives.

"Glad to see you two working on your next career," I said, closing my pack and hoisting it off the ground. "You can call yourselves Circus Pest Control."

They both ignored me, and Nitro walked to the tree to retrieve his knives. One of the spiders remained on a blade when he pulled it out of the trunk, and he started to carry the still twitching arachnid back to where Spider was standing.

"I will shoot you in your muscle-bound ass," Spider said when he saw what was coming his way.

"Knock it off, girls," I growled, figuring it was time for some adult intervention before things got out of hand.

We spent another ten minutes getting ready, then set out in the same movement pattern we'd used the previous day. Less than half a mile from camp, we all faltered and looked around when a gorilla screamed in the forest. The light was fading, and mist was settling on the forest floor, making it hard to see much of anything either with the naked eye or night vision. The ape sounded like it was only a few yards off the trail we were using, but other than the one scream, we didn't hear anything else.

The camp of the warlord not involved in the power struggle was twelve miles away from ours. We had to avoid a couple of villages as we moved through the dark jungle, but we were quiet and passed unnoticed. None of the locals were out, and I assumed word of what was happening had spread, and everyone who wasn't directly involved was hunkering down for the night.

Almost three hours later we were within half a mile of our target. I called a halt to the main group and sent Poon, and an Aussie named Wills, ahead to recon and give us some real time intel. Wills was a typical SF type, average height and a build that would be stocky if he didn't burn about eight thousand calories a day being a badass operator. They disappeared into the dark mist without a sound.

An hour later, Wills returned solo. Poon had found a nice sniping position and had settled in for the duration. With a stick, the Aussie drew a map of the compound in the dirt and used rocks and sticks to represent buildings and static guards. Well... guard. They only had one guy out keeping an eye on things. Everyone else was settled in.

Making a plan on the fly, I took a moment to contact Poon on the radio and verify nothing had changed. With confirmation that everything was still the same, I issued orders, and the group spread into the jungle in the direction of the compound. I sent Doc with Wills, who would escort him to Poon's position before moving on to his assignment. Delker got paired up with Two Step, who would keep a close eye on the agent for me.

Once we were all in place, forming a perimeter around the camp, I gave the order for Poon to take out the guard. He did so with a single shot, the man flipping onto his back in the mud when the top of his head was blown off. I gave it a ten count to make sure no one in the compound had seen or heard anything, then issued the *GO* order when all remained quiet.

There were four mud and straw buildings, very much like the village we'd raided the previous night. With Poon on overwatch and two of Lucas's men keeping an eye on our backs, we flowed out of the darkness and approached the quiet camp. We were going to make entry one structure at a time, four of us going in while the remainder of the joint team made sure no one came out of any of the other huts.

I was leading the assault team, Lucas, Spider and Smyth coming with me. We would make entry into the first building, eliminate any of the warlord's soldiers we found, then move on to the next. Doing this quietly was my goal. I didn't want a firefight to erupt and alert the other villages in the area.

I wasn't worried about any of them coming to our target's aid. I wanted to wipe out this compound and not leave a trace. The more fear and uncertainty that could be instilled in the other camps, the better it would be for us.

It wasn't that late, but the camp was quiet. No loud voices from men drinking and telling stories of their latest act of bravery or sexual conquest. No radios playing. Had they gone to bed early? Only one way to find out.

16

Lucas, Smyth and Spider were stacked up behind me. We were hard against the exterior wall of one of the huts, each man with his left hand on the shoulder of the man immediately in front of him. I listened hard at the sheet-covered doorway, hearing the subtle sounds of several men breathing.

Not the nervous intake of air a man makes when he's waiting for a fight, but the slow, steady sound of sleep. I was surprised, but also grateful. If they were all asleep, our jobs would be much easier.

Extending the muzzle of my rifle, I parted the curtain and stepped through the opening. I quickly moved to my left, rifle up as I scanned through the night vision for a target. Lucas followed and broke to the right, then Smyth followed me as Spider stayed with Lucas.

Looking around, I saw eight men sprawled out on blankets, sound asleep. Our entry into the hut hadn't disturbed them. I also saw half a dozen large cardboard boxes ripped open, their contents spilled carelessly onto the dirt floor. Red Cross relief packages, intended for the starving people these guys were terrorizing.

Hunter's Rain

Food wrappers were everywhere, just thrown down when the contents had been consumed. These eight had dined well, ignoring the medical supplies that had also been in the shipment. In the two seconds I spent checking over the mess, I could tell they'd eaten enough food to feed a family of four for a week.

Issuing instructions with hand signals, I let my rifle hang on its sling and drew my Ka-Bar knife. Lucas did as well, Spider and Smyth keeping watch over the room with their rifles. Starting at the outside edges, we worked our way in, killing each man in his sleep with a thrust of the blade after clamping a hand over his mouth to prevent him from calling out as he died.

It didn't take long, then we wiped our blades clean and went outside. I'd just killed four men in less than two minutes. I should feel something, but I didn't. Not now. I would later. They'd visit me late at night. But even then I wouldn't regret what I'd done. Not when they had chosen to prey on the weak and defenseless.

Nitro was close when I emerged into the fresh air, and he signaled all was still quiet. I nodded and led the way to the next hut. We repeated the process, killing six more. The third building held eleven, and all went without a whisper. Approaching the final structure, I could hear two distinct voices, speaking in a singsong dialect.

I signed to the others that I was hearing voices and Smyth stepped up, asking to go through the door first. After his demonstration before we'd left camp, I had a pretty good idea what he had in mind. Nodding, I slipped in behind him and placed my left hand on his shoulder when I felt Lucas's on mine. That was his signal that the team behind him was ready.

He had a throwing knife in each hand, stepping through the curtain and launching them so hard there were audible impacts when they struck their targets. As soon as he released the blades he went left and I went right, running directly into a large, shirtless man. My rifle was up, the muzzle contacting his chest when we collided and I pulled the trigger and pumped several rounds into his body.

For a moment he stood there, staring at me in shock, then blood trickled out of his mouth and he collapsed to the dirt. There weren't any more men in the building, which was the largest of the four. I glanced at the two Smyth had killed, noting the nearly impeccable placement of the blades.

Spider hissed at me from the far side of the room, and I went over to look at what he'd found. Stacks upon stacks of Red Cross and UN relief packages. Enough for a decent sized village to have food and medicine for at least a month.

"Reaper one is clear," I called on the radio. "Reaper five, sitrep?"

"Five. Area is clear," Poon answered immediately.

"One copies," I answered. "Reaper four, bring your passenger in."

Two Step acknowledged and in less than a minute the curtain parted, and he and Delker stepped into the building.

"That our guy?" I asked, clicking on a small flashlight and shining it on the face of one of the dead man dressed like every tin-pot dictator the world has seen.

"Yep. That's him," he said a minute later after finding an image on his sat phone and comparing it to the corpse.

"Spider, get some help and move all these boxes out into the middle of the compound. The locals might not come in here looking, but if they see them out in the open, they'll come take them," I said.

He nodded, scooped several into his arms and headed outside. Smyth followed suit, Lucas, Delker and I moving into the open air. I turned my head at the sound of distant automatic weapons fire.

"Reaper five, where's that coming from?" I asked Poon over the radio. In his elevated sniping position, he would have a better view of the surrounding area.

"Couple of klicks to the east," he answered right away. "Also a couple of fires just started."

"Village?" I asked Delker.

"There's one in that direction. Maybe three hundred people." He answered.

"Form up. We're moving," I transmitted on the comm channel.

It had taken me all of two seconds to make the decision. This was what we were here for. Stop these assholes.

"Where we going, boss?" Nitro asked as he placed an armload of aid packages on the dirt.

"Village east of here under attack," I said, impatiently waiting as everyone scrambled into position.

Twenty seconds later we were ready, just waiting for Poon-tang and Doc. Five more seconds and they burst out of the brush at a run and joined up with us.

Hunter's Rain

I couldn't remember the name of the Aussie trooper that reminded me of Hulk Hogan, so I just called him Hulk. He had been Lucas's point man the entire time they'd been in-country and knew his way around. Leading us directly into the jungle, he held a southerly course for a few hundred yards before picking up a narrow trail and turning due east.

As we moved, the sounds of occasional gunfire grew louder. Someone was still firing full auto, but they were using short bursts. I guessed this was soldiers mopping up a slaughter, and I pushed the team faster.

We covered the distance quickly, fanning out through the undergrowth as we approached the village. The thatched roofs of several small buildings were on fire, burning brightly in the dark. As we spread into a skirmish line, Poon found a location to his liking and took up position.

At the edge of a large clearing, I peered through the leaves of some tropical bush and cursed under my breath. Bodies were scattered everywhere. Men, women and children lay where they had been cut down by either gunfire or machetes. Even at this distance, I could smell the stink of blood, bowels and bladders over the acrid scent of burnt gunpowder.

This was the largest village I had seen so far, with close to fifty structures. Many were the mud and grass construction of the last couple of villages, but there were also some buildings that had been pieced together with wood and sheets of tin. Fire lit the whole area as everything that could burn had been set ablaze. It looked like one of Dante's levels of hell.

We were at the western edge of town and there was no movement within visual range, but weapons fire and screams of terror and pain were coming from deeper in. I issued an order over the radio, and as one we emerged from the jungle and began moving across the cleared ground.

I took the lead now, pausing at the first mud hut I came to. Its thatched grass roof had burned out and fallen inside. Several pairs of feet stuck out from under the debris, a couple sets of them very small. Stepping around the building I had to pick my way through a field of bodies. All of them had been violently torn open and spilled a lot of blood, which mixed with the mud where they came to rest. Not bothering to look, I knew my boots would be covered with the foul morass.

Flowing through the maze of the village, we avoided the heat and light of burning structures, sticking to the shadows as much as possible. The farther we progressed, the more bodies we encountered. I was beginning to question Delker's estimate of the number of residents. We had already encountered more than three hundred corpses, and I could see close to another hundred just ahead of us.

At what I guessed was the center of town, I got my first look at some of the attackers. All young men, wearing ragged clothing and carrying the ubiquitous AK-47. Some were grown, but many appeared to not yet be out of their teens. The older ones were in charge, the younger running from hut to hut and firing long bursts as they pushed through the flimsy doors.

Screams filled the air, many of them being cut off by the rattle of the attackers' weapons. The team was spread out around me, and all I needed to do to issue the order to go was to raise my rifle and start firing. Bodies spun to the bloody ground as our rounds found their mark. We quickly cleared the area and moved forward, checking buildings as we went to make sure an armed enemy didn't get missed to run around behind us.

I paused when I heard retching from my left. Looking, I saw Hulk standing outside a small mud hut. He was bent over, hands on his knees, taking big gulps of air. Changing directions, I moved to the door of the building he'd just exited.

"You don't want to go in there," he gasped.

No. I didn't. But I did anyway. One look and I froze in place, staring in horror.

The hut had been a nursery. Two women had been shot multiple times, their bodies just inside the door. But the horror was what had been done to the seven babies that were inside. Each had been beheaded, their tiny skulls stacked up into a pyramid that greeted you as you entered.

A wave of heat flushed from my chest up across my face. The team had noticed the detour and one by one each of the men stuck his head through the doorway and looked. Delker took several photos with his satellite phone before he ran out to throw up.

Exiting the shack, I looked at the faces around me and saw the same emotion I was feeling. Rage. Unstoppable rage. Anyone that could do something like this wasn't human and didn't deserve one ounce of mercy.

"Reaper five, adjust your position to the east end of town. No one leaves here alive," I called on the radio.

Poon acknowledged, and we set out with considerably less caution than we had exercised up until now. Letting your emotions come into play when going to battle is rarely a good idea. They cloud your mind and as a result, you make bad decisions that can get you or a teammate killed. But sometimes, despite years of training, they just can't be denied and you take them with you into the fight.

Anger fueled us as we resumed moving through the village. Rifles were fired, but they didn't satisfy the bloodlust that had been raised by the scene in the nursery. Soon we switched to knives and relentlessly pursued the poorly trained soldiers through the night. What was supposed to be a professional military interdiction became wholesale slaughter.

Throats were cut. Kidneys and hearts were stabbed. Bodies were slashed open by hate fueled hands. No quarter was given. We were merciless. We were death incarnate. We killed every attacker, washing the rage away with their blood. It was messy. It was horrifically brutal. When it was over, we all gathered in a large circle, panting like we'd just run a marathon.

Standing there in the mud, I looked around what was now a band of brothers. We'd crossed a line tonight. We hadn't been recruited and trained and sent into the field to let our emotions take over. To turn us into mindless killing machines. We were supposed to be professionals. But we were still human and had responded to some horrifically inhuman acts by the men we'd just slaughtered like cattle.

Hard eyes stared back at me as I scanned the face of each man. Nowhere did I see remorse. Only the black, soulless stare of men whose only desire was to kill more of the enemy. For several minutes we stood silent, each of us lost in our own thoughts. The rain picked up, washing our bodies clean of the blood and gore that stained us. But it couldn't cleanse our souls of what we'd seen. Finally, training took over and I started barking orders to get us ready to move.

We saved seventeen villagers that night. All of them young girls that had been rounded up. It didn't take a lot of imagination to figure out why. They stood in a tight group, staring at us, unsure what had just happened. Mad Max went to talk to them while Delker, Nitro and Two Step began cataloging the numbers. It's always seemed ridiculous to me, but the Army inevitably wants to know body counts.

17

It had been a long, somber hike back to our camp. Hulk led us down a myriad of game trails, and I was impressed with his ability to keep us on the right track in the dense mist and near total darkness. At least we had night vision and could maintain a decent rate of travel. Otherwise, we would have been moving at a snail's pace.

The joint team probably had close to one hundred and fifty combined years of experience as Special Forces Operators, but there was not a single one of us who hadn't been affected by what we'd found in the village. Sure, most of us had been in war-torn parts of the world and seen the horrors that only humans are capable of committing against their own species. But none of us had ever witnessed the complete callousness that had been demonstrated in the village nursery.

There was faint light on the eastern horizon when we arrived at our camp. Hulk, Nitro and Smyth moved ahead of the group as we approached. They made sure no one had come in while we were gone and left us any little surprises. Hulk called an *all clear* over the radio as the rest of us approached, and I was glad to sit down on a fallen tree and take a deep drink of water.

The first order of business was weapons maintenance, and as soon as a watch was posted, we all busied ourselves. Everyone was spread out, and the usual sarcastic barbs were missing, as no one spoke. I felt the same way, but began talking as I removed the bolt from my rifle for an inspection and cleaning.

"This kind of shit is why we're here," I said. My voice was contemplative, the only sound in the pre-dawn jungle other than the metallic clinks and clanks of firearms being worked on. "We knew this was going to be bad coming in. We've all seen some fucked up shit before. Make sure your heads are right by the time we go out tonight. Talk to your buddy. Do what you need to be ready to go."

A lot of heads around the camp nodded. These guys weren't newbies. They knew the drill. They were human, so, of course they were impacted, but they were also professional soldiers and would do what needed to be done.

"I really don't get this shit," Spider said from where he sat a few feet away from me.

"What?" I asked when he didn't continue.

"This is where I'm from," he said, pausing to purse his lips and blow a piece of debris from his rifle chamber. "Well, where my ancestors are from. How the fuck can my people do this kind of shit?"

Hunter's Rain

I was surprised. Spider had been my friend for ten years, and even though I'd never given it any conscious thought, I'd just assumed he was a descendant of slaves who had been brought to America. But the slavers had taken from the populations along the western coast of Africa. We were a long way from the coast. Too far.

"Didn't know that, did you?" He asked me.

"No. I didn't." I admitted.

"My great grandmother was a tribal princess. Wealthy family and all, at least by African standards. She was on a trip to Zanzibar with her father and met a Kenyan fisherman in the market. Love at first sight. Her father forced her to come home and forbade her to ever see the fisherman again.

"A month or so later he showed up at her village in the middle of the night, and she ran off with him. They ran for days, her father's men chasing them, but they escaped and settled in South Africa. Had my grandfather. He was a fisherman for a while, then became a merchant seaman. Happened to be in Hawaii when the Japanese bombed Pearl Harbor.

"His ship was one of a few civilian cargo vessels that were sunk in the attack, and with nothing except the clothes on his back, he lied about who he was and where he was from and managed to enlist in the US Army."

"How the hell did he pull that off?" Two Step interrupted.

Everyone that wasn't on watch had gathered around to hear Spider's story.

"This was 1941, and everyone was in a panic," Spider said. "There weren't computers or databases or anything like that. Hell, you only had ID back then if you had a driver's license, and you didn't even have one if you didn't own a car. Besides, if you were black in the 1940s, no one expected you to have any type of ID. Very different world then.

"Anyway, he joined up, and after a year as a cook was transferred to the 92nd Infantry Division and became a Buffalo Soldier. Fought in Italy. Was awarded a Silver Star and stayed in the Army. Met my grandmother in Alabama a year after he got home. He was at Fort McClellan, and she was a civilian worker who was bussed onto post every day to clean high-ranking officer's houses.

"They had my father ten months after they met. He grew up and was in the 1st Special Forces in Vietnam. My mom was a Navy nurse that took care of him on a hospital ship when he got shot up. I didn't know any of this until a couple of years ago.

My grandfather was dying, and I spent my leave with him, and he told me the story."

"You're fucking royalty?" Nitro asked, a shit-eating grin on his face.

"So which tribe was your great grandmother from?" I asked.

"The one doing all the killing," Spider said, erasing the grin on Nitro's face.

Silence descended over the camp. Each man studiously avoided looking at Spider, instead concentrating on reassembling his weapon.

"You alright?" I asked after several long moments of quiet.

"I'm right where I need to be," he said, releasing the bolt on his rifle and letting it slam into place.

"OK, then, Prince Spider," I said. "You've got first watch."

"Need me to carry your gun for you, Prince?" Nitro couldn't resist. "Wouldn't want the royal arms to get tired or anything."

"If you really want to carry something heavy, I've got to take a piss. Come along and hold it for me?" Spider shot back as he stood.

I was glad to hear him sounding more like his smart ass self.

"Nah. I didn't bring my glasses and tweezers this trip."

"Then how the hell do you find yours?" Spider grinned, flipped him off and headed for the edge of camp.

18

I took the mid-day watch after sleeping for a few hours. There was heavy overcast, muting the colors of the jungle, and a clinging mist coated everything with fine droplets of water. Looking at my surroundings as I watched and listened, I thought it should be cool, but it wasn't. We may have been up in the thinner air of the mountains, but we were still very close to the equator, and the temperature was up. Not hot like a lowland jungle, but warm enough to not match the visual.

Sitting at the eastern perimeter of our camp was a mountain that rose majestically, its peak disappearing into the clouds. Directly to my front and right, the ground dropped away into a broad river valley filled with the omnipresent white mist. It hugged the ground beneath the thick canopy of trees and made them appear to be growing out of cotton candy.

It was near the end of my watch when I picked up the sound of movement on the mountain slope above me. I was well concealed in the spreading branches of some kind of bush that looked just like a silk houseplant my mother had bought when I was a small child. Broad, dark green leaves with a lighter stripe around the perimeter. They were supported by thick branches that were used as a highway by an enormous variety of insects and lizards.

Cautiously, I turned my head in the direction of the sound and slowly brought my rifle to my shoulder. I didn't see anything but continued to hear the occasional crack of a branch as whoever it was moved through the foliage. The mist and heavy vegetation obscured my view, and I had to rely on my ears to follow their track.

My heart rate jumped a little as the sounds continued to approach, but I was comfortable with the position I was in. Wearing jungle camouflage fatigues with my face blacked out, I was invisible amongst the deeper shade of the plant. I considered calling an alert on the radio but held off for the moment. I didn't have eyes on a threat, plus I didn't want to make any sound that would give away my hiding place.

Another branch cracked at a different location, and I realized there was more than one intruder. Maintaining complete stillness, I scanned across the area by only moving my eyes. I thought I detected a hint of movement to the extreme right, but when I cut my vision in that direction, I didn't see anything. I caught my breath when there was a low grunt to my left.

Turning my head and bringing my rifle to bear, I was momentarily taken aback when I saw a gorilla only thirty yards away. The animal was standing at the base of a small tree, reaching up and pulling down young, green branches. One of them snapped with a crack that was muted by the mist, and it began stripping off the tender leaves and bark with its teeth. I was amazed and excited to be watching as it fed, apparently unaware of my presence. Or perhaps unconcerned.

It was large with long powerful arms. At least as heavy as I am, but if I had to guess it probably had a good fifty pounds on me. I didn't know a lot about the great apes but did know they were significantly stronger than a human and could rip me limb from limb if so inclined. Regardless, I sat perfectly still and enjoyed the show. Until there was a deep grunt from my far right, close enough that I could hear the expulsion of air that went along with it.

Turning my head, I froze when I spotted a massive ape staring directly at me from no more than ten yards away. This had to be a male, and it was a truly impressive specimen. Four hundred pounds if it was an ounce, it stood on all fours with the weight of its massive upper body resting on huge arms. I could see whitish fur covering its spine and *silverback* flashed through my mind.

The gorilla's head was enormous. A face about the size of a human, black and leathery with a large skull extending well above its forehead. He grunted again, then snorted without ever taking his eyes off of me.

The eyes were deeply set under a heavily ridged brow and looking into them I could see the intelligence of the creature. It was like looking into another human's eyes, not an animal's. To say it was a life-changing experience would be overly dramatic, but it was still profound. These weren't the dull eyes of a gorilla in captivity at the zoo. These were bright, thoughtful and made me feel something more primal than I ever have.

I've spent a lot of time around animals throughout my life, mostly dogs and horses. You can see the intelligence in both as well as the love and loyalty in a dog, but this was more like looking at another person. I'll never know what the gorilla saw in my eyes. Perhaps he thought I was just another ape, or maybe he recognized the difference between our species. Perhaps he even thought I was a less intelligent ape.

Either way, he must have been satisfied that I didn't pose a threat to him or any of the others I could now see moving through the jungle behind him. He was the largest of the group, the others probably being females as well as several no larger than a small child. It was a family, and he was making sure the interloper didn't do anything to harm any of them.

Hunter's Rain

If he charged, he could have covered the ground between us faster than I could have brought my rifle around. I'd committed the cardinal sin of not keeping my rifle pointed in the direction I was looking, and now it was off target. Not that it would have done any good. I didn't think anything less than Poon's .50 caliber rifle would stop him without a lot of well-placed shots. Certainly, more than I'd be able to fire before he ripped my arms out of their sockets and pounded my bloody corpse into the mud.

But I didn't need to worry. As the family passed out of visual range, he snorted again before casually turning and following them. For such a large animal, he was graceful, seemingly moving without effort. And he was deceptively fast. In a few seconds he vanished into the mist, and I couldn't even hear him moving. I released a breath I hadn't realized I was holding, a smile breaking out across my face.

"Bloody hell, that was something!"

I jumped when Lucas spoke right behind me. I'd been so enthralled with the ape that I hadn't been paying attention and had failed to hear him approach.

"Holy shit," I grinned at him. "How long were you there?"

"I was coming up when he suddenly appeared right in front of you," he said, settling into the bush next to me. "Stopped about thirty meters away when I saw him. Thought you were dead. I didn't have a shot."

"I didn't either," I admitted, still smiling despite myself. "Wow. That's something that doesn't happen every day. Could you see his eyes?"

"No, not from where I was. All I could tell was that he was looking right at you."

"Fucking amazing!"

I gushed like an excited child. I should have been maintaining noise discipline.

"My watch," Lucas said, smiling back at me.

I nodded and slowly wormed my way through the branches and stood up straight. I turned and looked in the direction the family of gorillas had gone. No sight or sound of them other than several branches on the ground that had been stripped clean.

"Incredible," I mumbled to myself as I began walking back to camp.

My original plan had been to get some more sleep before tonight's activities, but after my encounter, there was no way that was going to happen.

19

We set out a couple of hours after dark. It was raining. Again. Not so much rain as a steady mist falling out of the night sky, soaking everything. The ground was mud, every leaf and branch coated with water. It was impossible to not at least brush against the foliage, and a fresh shower would rain down and add to the misery every time I came into contact with a bush or tree.

Hulk was on point, leading us through the forest, but we didn't have a specific destination. Tonight was patrol night. Check the areas where the warlords liked to operate and see if any of their men were out causing trouble. We were hunting.

It had been no more than an hour since we'd left our camp when Spider tapped my shoulder and tilted his head towards Delker. I looked and saw him calling for a halt. A quick mumble over the radio and all of the men melded deeper into the bush and took up defensive positions. Moving to crouch next to the CIA man, I shoved my NVGs off my face and growled at him.

"What?"

"Text message from one of my assets," he mumbled. At least he remembered how to stay quiet in the field. "Take a look."

He handed me his sat phone, and I peered at the message on the screen.

"Who's Wazi?" I asked, handing the phone back.

"Worst of the worst," he said. "Fucker's probably killed as many villagers as all the other warlords combined."

I looked at him for a moment, then put a call out to Hulk. A few seconds later, he suddenly appeared out of the darkness and knelt down next to us with a curious expression on his face.

"Show him," I said to Delker, who held the handset out so Hulk could see the screen.

"Know where that is?" I asked.

"'Bout ten klicks to the southwest," he said. "But, we gotta go around a mountain to get there, so closer to twenty."

I thanked him and called Lucas, asking him to come to my location. He appeared as suddenly as Hulk had, taking a long drink of water as he knelt.

"Heard of Wazi?" I asked.

"Been looking for that bloody cocksucker since we got here," he said, his eyes lighting up in excitement. "Why?"

Hunter's Rain

"Delker got a tip. We know where he is."

"How far?"

"Twenty klicks, give or take," I answered. "Five hours in this shit. Minimum. Worth it?"

"Absolutely," Lucas said, nodding for emphasis.

"How big's his army?" I asked, looking back and forth between Delker and Lucas.

"Big," Delker said.

"Very," Lucas said. "From what the villagers have told us, he's got at least a hundred men, and they're well armed."

I stared off into the darkness for a moment, thinking. If the warlord really had over a hundred-man army, we were seriously outnumbered. But, this was why we were here. We weren't paid to avoid a fight just because we were outnumbered.

"Pass the word," I said, making my decision. "We're going to go see if we can't fuck up his night."

Lucas grinned and disappeared as silently as he'd arrived. I nodded at Delker and moved back onto the narrow game trail we'd been following. Quickly, the rest of the soldiers emerged from the foliage and then we were on our way.

Hulk kept us going north for a few minutes, then we made a sharp turn to the southwest when the jungle thinned slightly. We were no longer on a game trail and quickly spread out to keep good spacing between us. That meant we were far enough away from each other that if one of us was attacked, the others weren't in immediate danger. But, we were close enough together that we could maintain visual contact and be able to jump into a fight in the blink of an eye.

We pushed on through the night, stopping once to drink and wolf down some MREs. The rain had changed from a gentle mist to an outright deluge. Each of us was soaked to the skin, water squishing out of our boots with each step. It was absolutely miserable weather, but at least it was keeping all of the bad guys at home. We didn't see or hear a single sign of life, other than the nocturnal jungle animals.

There were plenty of those in the trees over our heads. They hooted, howled, screeched and made about every other noise imaginable. The rain didn't seem to have dampened their spirits in the least. Occasionally, when I'd look up, I'd catch a glimpse of a sinuous shape leaping from one tree to another, but couldn't identify the animal through the night vision.

Finally, after a long trek along the banks of a swiftly running river, we turned into a small valley and came to a stop. Less than a klick ahead were dozens of fires spread out across the jungle floor. Everyone had gone to ground when we stopped, and I cautiously made my way forward to where Hulk knelt behind a massive bush. Lucas fell in step, joining me.

"That it?" I asked Hulk, who was holding a pair of magnifiers up to his NVGs.

"Yep. That's them," he said without looking away.

"What is this place?"

"Used to be a Catholic mission," he said. "Trying to help orphans and unwanted kids. Wazi killed the priest and gave the nuns to his men. When they were done with them... well, you don't want to know."

"No. I don't," I said. "What can you see?"

"Not much," he said, then lifted his arm and pointed to an area to the right of our target. "Thinking we circle around onto that high ground. We'll be able to get a good look at the fuckers, and I'm betting that's outside any pickets they've got set up."

"Get us there," I said without hesitation.

Lucas passed the word over the radio and less than a minute later we started moving again.

But, this was slow and careful movement. We were close to the enemy, and couldn't afford to make any mistakes that would give away our approach. Each step was cautious, testing the ground before weight was transferred to that foot. Senses were hyper alert, listening and looking for anything and everything.

It was half an hour before we made it to the low ridge that Hulk had identified. Everyone knew what they were doing and quickly spread out in a long line that overlooked the abandoned mission. Squirming beneath a rain-soaked bush, I poked my head through the opposite side and took a long look at our target.

The mission was nothing like one would expect to see if they'd lived in the southwestern United States. There were no soaring arches or stuccoed walls, or a bell tower thrust high into the air. Not here in Africa. Instead, it was simply a large, square structure that had been built of mud and straw and some scraps of wood. The roof was low, constructed of some sort of thin logs covered with more straw. Maybe it kept the incessant rain out, but I doubted it.

Over twenty vehicles were parked haphazardly around a muddy courtyard. Most were the ubiquitous Toyota Hilux, but there were a few military vehicles that had been built in the Soviet Union. Not surprising, especially considering the goddamn Russians had always thought interfering in Africa was another way to poke America in the eye.

The fires we'd seen from the entrance to the valley were in rusting, fifty-five gallon drums. Each had a crude rain shield fashioned from lengths of metal that suspended a flat piece of steel a couple of feet above the flames. There were apparently more of these inside the building as I could see flickering light coming through the doorway and a couple of small, high windows.

Tarps had been tied to the vehicles and strung between them, creating semi-dry areas for the men to sleep. The rain wasn't falling directly on them, but I was sure that water was seeping its way into their bedding. But, they were probably used to it. Around the perimeter of the camp, four bored looking men were walking guard.

Well, they really didn't qualify as men. Each was painfully young. Probably no more than thirteen or fourteen. Three of the four were shirtless and shoeless, but they all carried AK-47s with bandoliers of spare magazines slung around their scrawny bodies.

"I count eighty-three, eight three, sleeping and four sentries," I mumbled to Poon over the radio.

Dirk Patton

As soon as we'd arrived, he'd found the highest ground he could and set up with his sniper rifle. The optics he was using were far superior to what I had.

"Confirm eight three plus four," his voice came over my earpiece a minute later.

I stayed where I was for another five minutes, looking over the entire area and deciding how we were going to proceed. Plan in my head, I crawled backward and moved farther back into the bush. With Poon and Doc keeping watch over the camp, I called everyone together and quickly outlined what we were going to do.

As I passed out assignments, each man met my eyes and nodded that he understood his job. Soon, only Lucas and Delker remained. Lucas and I would enter from opposite ends of the camp when we began our assault, but I intentionally hadn't included the CIA agent.

"What do you want me to do?" He asked.

"Stick with Doc," I said. "Poon's going to be busy, and someone needs to keep an eye on him."

He didn't like it, but we'd reached a mutual understanding that didn't include him joining us in combat. I wasn't about to trust someone who hadn't been in combat for years. He might remember what to do and how to do it, but knowing something and being trained and prepared were two very different things. He stared at me for a long beat, and for a moment I thought he was going to argue. But, he only nodded and moved off to find Doc.

The men were already in place, ready to go. Lucas and I looked at each other, then he nodded, and we headed for either end of the ridge. It took me a couple of minutes to get in place, prone on the rain-saturated ground.

I wasn't going to bitch. The same weather that had made the twenty klick march through the jungle so miserable was now working in our favor. The sentries were bored, but they were also tired of being out in the deluge. I'd noted that each of them was just trudging along with his head bowed, staring at the ground directly in front of his feet. A pink unicorn could probably have walked by, and none of them would have seen it.

The other advantage was the constant white noise produced by the hiss of raindrops falling onto the ground and foliage. There was no way they'd hear us coming until it was too late, and it was also going to keep the sleeping men unaware of our presence.

I took a final look at the camp, then called Poon on the radio to double check that nothing had changed. With his confirmation that we were ready to go, I rose into a crouch, rifle up and ready, and issued the order to execute the assault.

20

I hadn't even taken a step when Poon's voice came over the radio. He called for everyone to hold, repeating himself three times to make sure the message was heard. Dropping back into cover, I immediately requested a headcount, breathing a silent sigh of relief after each man responded that he was holding position.

"Poon, what'd you see?" I asked after the final response.

"Two X-Rays approaching from the south."

Fuck. Where the hell had these guys come from?

"Copy," I said, swiveling around to see in the indicated direction.

It didn't take long for me to spot the movement. Two men, somewhat better dressed than the guards, emerged from the edge of the jungle and strolled into the courtyard without a care in the world. The closest sentry noticed them but ignored their passage. They made their way around the edge of the building and disappeared through the door.

"Everyone hold," I transmitted. "Spider. Nitro. Go take a peek and see what they were doing."

Spider acknowledged the order, then the radio went silent. Rain continued to fall while I waited for their report. Hidden deep within a bush, I watched the guards as they slogged through sticky mud. While I was loathe to admit it, I was actually impressed. As young and miserable as these guys were, they were doing their jobs. That didn't so much speak for them as it did the warlord and the senior men directly beneath him. They had definitely instilled some discipline into their ragtag army.

"Boss, you'd better come see this."

Spider's voice in my ear made me forget all about the guards.

"Copy. Coming to you," I answered, slithering behind the ridge before standing up.

It took me several minutes to make my way through the dense foliage. Lucas had joined up with me as I passed where he was hidden. We passed an ancient bulldozer, then stepped into the clearing where Spider waited for us. Nitro was behind a tree, keeping watch on a narrow path that ran down from the mission.

Hunter's Rain

I've smelled a lot of horrible things during my time in uniform, but the stench in the clearing was right up there with the worst of the worst. Even in the pouring rain, it was bad. I couldn't imagine what it would be like on a hot, humid day, baking under the sun. Spider looked at me, and I could see an expression of anger on his face.

"In there," he said, gesturing at a large pit.

It was behind him, and he didn't turn to look when he pointed it out. Lucas and I stepped forward, moving past him and coming to a stop at the edge. Staring, I was speechless.

"Bloody fucking hell," Lucas breathed.

The pit was deep, with vertical sides. In it, heaped like cordwood, were rotting corpses. It was impossible to get a count, the way they were stacked, but there must have been at least three hundred of them. Of the ones near the top, most showed damage from machetes. Limbs cut off. Heads severed. Bodies sliced open. Genitals removed and stuffed into gaping mouths.

As I kept looking, I realized that some of the corpses appeared to have barely been older than a toddler, while a few of the heads were covered with gray hair. All the ages in between were also well represented. Turning, I saw a spot a few feet to my right where tree branches had been placed on the ground, overlooking the pit, so someone could stand there without being in the mud. Walking over, a different smell hit me.

Leaning out, I looked down at a large pile of human excrement that rested on top of several bodies. The goddamn warlord and his army were using the mass grave for a latrine. Heaping one last indignity on the people they'd slaughtered.

I looked around when Lucas reappeared next to me.

"I thought the nursery was bad," he said. "But, this..."

"It was bad," I said, shaking my head. "Maybe worse than this. But this is the same brand of sick shit. Why? What the fuck's the point? I get the adult males, but why children?"

"Because they grow up and go looking for vengeance."

We both turned to see Spider standing behind us, well away from the pit. He looked more distraught than I'd ever seen him.

"No women," Lucas said softly.

"What?" I asked, turning to look at him.

"In the pit," he said. "No women."

Hunter's Rain

I started checking bodies and soon realized he was right. Every single one was male. I was afraid I knew what had been done with the females.

Something inside me clicked at that moment. Despite my chosen profession, I'm actually a pretty easy going guy. It takes a lot to get me mad. But, I was beyond mad. This wasn't something that one human did to another. This wasn't even something an animal would do. This was pure evil. There was no other word I could come up with.

We'd lost it the night before, and I'd thought that would be a one-time thing. Wanted it to be. We weren't supposed to be executioners. We were supposed to be hunters. But that didn't matter. Standing here in the rain, staring at the mutilated corpses, all that mattered was that we didn't let any of the men who'd done this survive the night.

"Reaper five, copy?" I called on the radio through clenched teeth.

"Go," Poon answered immediately.

"Send agent man to my location."

I didn't know if it mattered, but I wanted Delker to document this. Take it back home and make sure the people who decided whether or not to intercede in foreign countries got to see what I had seen. I just wished they were all standing here in the rain with me. Seeing and smelling and feeling it for themselves.

He arrived within a couple of minutes and stood in mute horror between Lucas and me.

"Did you know about this?" I asked.

He shook his head without saying anything.

"Get some photos," I said. "You've got one minute, then we're going to go kill every one of those motherfuckers."

He swallowed hard and moved closer to the pit. Turning on an infrared light, he aimed it at the bodies and started snapping photos with an IR camera.

"Lucas, spread the word. The men need to know what we found. There's no mercy tonight."

He nodded, then after another long look into the pit, turned and disappeared into the jungle. I watched Delker reposition himself a couple of times to get different angles, then he clicked off the light and tucked his equipment away and came to stand next to me.

Five minutes later I was back in position. Delker was back with Doc and Poon. I was confident everyone was cocked and locked, but still performed a quick check over the radio to make sure. When the last man acknowledged he was ready, I gave the execute order. Four of us, two American and two Australian, broke away from the main team and flowed through the jungle without a sound.

Spider and I were the yanks, Lucas and Hulk the Aussies. We all moved with our rifles to our shoulders, spreading out slightly as we stalked the four roving guards. Each of us paused at the edge of the courtyard, lowering our weapons and drawing knives. A second later, Poon's voice over the radio let us know there was still no movement other than our targets. That was our *go* signal.

Stepping beneath the branches of a small tree, I moved behind one of the sentries as he slowly slogged past. His head was down and shoulders hunched against the steady downpour. He may have been walking his post, but he was oblivious to anything that wasn't directly in front of his feet.

The kid was several inches taller than me and almost skeletally thin. Nothing much more than skin stretched tightly over his bones. His arms, legs and neck were extremely long, the appearance exaggerated because he was so skinny. He looked like he should be running up and down a basketball court rather than trudging through mud with an AK slung over his bony shoulders and a three-foot machete swinging from a belt made of rope.

I moved swiftly, Ka-Bar knife held low and ready in my right hand. It was essential that this guy went down silently and didn't have an opportunity to alert the sleeping men. We were seriously outnumbered, which would be a real problem if we got into a firefight.

Closing from behind, I got a feel for how tall he really was. I'm a couple of inches over six feet, but this guy was every bit of six inches taller than me, if not a little more. What I was going to do is much easier when the target is the same height, or shorter. It's awkward at best when he towers over you.

All of these thoughts flashed through my head as I closed the final three feet. Snaking my left arm up and around his throat, I levered him backward with my forearm. As he came back, I shifted so his neck was in the bend of my elbow and clamped down on his trachea as I thrust the eight-inch blade deep into his kidney.

There had been an instant of resistance before the knife pierced his body, and in that brief moment I got a feel for how strong he was. He'd twisted to the side, lifting my boots free of the mud, but a strike to the kidney is one of the surest ways to immediately incapacitate a man. As the blade sliced in, his body was thrown into shock, and all resistance ceased. Turning the blade, I stabbed in a second time as I maintained the pressure on his throat. I didn't think he'd be able to cry out but wasn't going to take the risk. Slowly, I lowered him to the ground, releasing my hold as his heart stopped.

Returning my knife to its sheath after wiping it clean on the dead man's ratty shorts, I brought my suppressed rifle around and looked for the rest of my team. I saw Spider first, standing over a corpse, then quickly located Lucas and Hulk. All of the sentries were down. Knowing Poon would be watching me through his thermal scope, I raised my hand and signaled for the start of our assault. A second later, his voice came over the radio.

The rest of the team appeared silently out of the darkness of the jungle. Any sound they may have made was completely masked by the constant hiss of the heavy rain. The sadistic little gods of war must have taken pity on us tonight. I couldn't have asked for any better weather to operate in.

As one, we moved forward with rifles up and selecting targets. Each man carried a sound suppressed weapon, and we'd taken the precaution of switching to subsonic ammunition. A suppressor to muffle the report of a rifle being fired is only half the battle. Bullets that travel faster than the speed of sound will create a miniature sonic boom, just like a fighter jet exceeding the sound barrier.

To be as quiet as possible, specialty ammunition is used to keep the speed down while still delivering a knockout punch on a target. Everything worked exactly as designed. As we began firing on the sleeping men, all I could hear over the rain was the faint, muted clacking of rifle bolts cycling.

We started at the outside edge of the camp, moving forward in a line. Men jumped and twitched as our rounds found their bodies. We were invisible in the darkness. Deathly silent. Just like the mythical creature who comes for you when your time is up, we took their lives without them ever knowing they were in danger. Tonight, we were all Reapers.

21

We pushed on, staying silent. It was slow work, maintaining noise discipline and making sure we didn't miss a sleeping soldier and leave an enemy to our rear. We advanced beyond the outermost ring of the camp, having killed perhaps a third of the men, when there was a sudden shout from far to my right. It was cut off immediately, but the damage had been done. Within seconds, heads began popping up in that general vicinity. Before they could be put down, an AK-47 started chattering. I heard the crack of a bullet then the rifle fell silent.

"Shooter down," Poon said over the radio, sounding calm and steady.

It would have been nice if it had been that simple, but that short burst of full-auto fire had woken all of the men we hadn't already shot. Shouts rose from all around, then more enemy rifles began firing. There was no retreating at this point. All that was left to do was put every one of them down before they had a chance to organize.

I transmitted one word that the entire team had already been briefed on. It told them we were going to keep fighting. Push ahead for our primary target, the warlord. Falling back wasn't an option.

We were still heavily outnumbered, despite all of the damage we'd already done.

If we retreated, it would simply give their commanders time to organize the men and come after us. We'd bloodied their nose, now it was time to finish the job. More AKs began firing, but I was unable to hear our answering shots. That didn't worry me. And, it still gave us a slight edge. But, we needed to press that advantage.

I shot two men who were scrambling out from beneath a tarp stretched between two vehicles, then had to dive onto the ground to avoid fire that started up from beneath an adjacent vehicle. As I crawled for the cover of a small truck, mud fountained into the air next to my head as the shooter tried to zero in on me. Rolling into shelter, I ripped a grenade off my vest, yanked the pin and lobbed it towards my attacker.

Shouting a warning over the radio, I spun away before it could detonate and perforate me with metal fragments. A couple of seconds later the blast rattled my teeth, and I leapt to my feet and charged forward, burning down three more men who were trying to draw a bead on Spider. I turned to the other side, coming face to face with a naked man aiming a large pistol at my head.

I was still bringing my rifle up, time stretching out as I watched his finger begin to tighten on the trigger. Throwing myself to the side, trying to avoid the bullet, I had an instant to think that I was about to die. Our eyes were locked as I fell, the muzzle tracking my face. The man smiled, revealing a mouthful of gold capped teeth, then his head exploded. Hot blood and brain matter sprayed across my face as his corpse flopped into the mud.

"Took your sweet fuckin' time, Poon," I said, jumping back to my feet and running forward.

"You're welcome, sweetie," he drawled.

The firefight lasted another five minutes. The side I'd taken was more heavily populated and as the Aussies mopped up their area, they collapsed in and helped me, Spider, Nitro and Two Step put down the last of the resistance.

Lucas, Hulk and Smyth had entered the building when they'd seen we had things mostly under control. I'd heard them on the radio as they cleared rooms, but since they weren't screaming for help, I hadn't paid any attention to them.

Finally, the last soldier went down and silence settled over the battlefield, broken only by the incessant rain. I immediately put a call out for everyone to check in with their status. Somehow, I'd managed to come out the other side of the fight without so much as a scratch. That didn't mean the rest of my team had.

Everyone, other than the three who'd gone into the building, responded. That was the good news. I hadn't lost anyone. But, there were several injuries. One as minor as a turned ankle, but Two Step and Mad Max had both taken bullets. Max had taken a round through his left hand and was in a lot of pain, and Two Step had somehow managed to get shot in the ass. Not straight in, mind you, but from the side. The bullet had bored a neat tunnel through his left ass cheek, missed his asshole by a, well an ass hair, then continued on through his right one. It would have almost been funny if the exit wound wasn't the size of my fist.

He was being cared for, and I was growing concerned that none of the men who'd gone inside had responded. Waving Nitro and Spider to follow, I headed for the door as I put out another call. This time, Hulk answered.

"Don't know where Lucas is," he said. "We had a bit of a party and got separated."

I'd reached the door by now and didn't bother yelling at him to find Lucas. I'd deal with that in person.

We entered the building fast and low, spreading out in the main room. I snapped my rifle up, very nearly drilling a round through Hulk's head when he suddenly appeared in an interior doorway.

Hunter's Rain

"What the fuck are you doing?" I hissed, walking towards him. "Where's Lucas?"

"You need to see this," he said without answering my second question.

I followed him into an adjacent room and pulled to a stop. A pair of kerosene lanterns hung from the ceiling, casting a dancing, yellow glow across the straw-covered dirt floor. In the far corner, Smyth stood next to several young girls who huddled in terror. None of them wore a stitch of clothing.

Along the front of the room, nearly three dozen pairs of shackles were bolted to the wall. A few were empty, that amount corresponding to the number of girls Smyth was guarding. But, far more still secured the wrists of girls and women that ranged in age from pre-teen to grandmothers. They were also completely nude and lay on the filthy straw, their arms held over their heads by the restraints. And they were all dead.

"What the fuck?" Nitro breathed from right behind me.

"Later," I snapped, anger surging through me. "Smyth, stay here and watch them. The rest of you, find Lucas. Now!"

We spread out, and I quickly realized the building was larger than it had initially appeared.

There were dead soldiers that belonged to Wazi in every room I passed through, and even though I was worried about my friend, I was pissed. He damn well knew better than to have charged into this building without adequate backup. He should have waited, and all of us would have come in. But, the three Aussies had taken care of business. There had been a fairly large contingent of bad guys, and it looked like they'd gotten all of them.

I'd been calling Lucas on the radio as I searched, but he wasn't responding. I was starting to think the worst had happened, then I moved close to a door and heard a pounding noise. The sound of fists on flesh. Normally, I'd hold in place and call for at least one more shooter to go in with me. But, Lucas unaccounted for and not answering my calls was anything but normal.

Rifle up, I put my back against the wall to the side of the opening and listened for a moment. Darting my head forward and pulling it back almost instantly, I got a brief glimpse of a figure on the far side of the room. It was hunched over something on the floor, wailing away on it. Well, that was the noise I was hearing.

Rolling around the door jamb, I quickly scanned the entire room through my rifle scope. Other than the man I'd already seen, nothing was moving. There was no furniture, just another dirt floor that was sparsely covered with old, moldy straw.

Rifle on the man who was still pounding, I pushed my night vision goggles up and clicked on a weapon mounted flashlight. It was brilliant in the darkness, and I immediately recognized Lucas. He was on his knees, back to me, arms raising and falling like trip hammers as he pummeled an unmoving man.

Taking another look around, I dashed forward. Reaching for Lucas's shoulder, I paused when I saw what he'd done. The man on the floor was on his back, and other than black skin, there wasn't much I could recognize. His face had been reduced to nothing more than a bloody pulp, and his chest was caved in from the damage Lucas continued to inflict.

Letting my rifle hang down, I placed my hand on my friend's shoulder and spoke his name. He didn't react. Didn't seem to be aware of my presence or touch. Just continued to pound on the dead man with his bloody hands. Kneeling, I wrapped him up from behind, gently speaking to him as I pulled him away from the corpse.

"Come on, mate. You got the bastard. He's gone. Let's get out of here."

Lucas didn't resist, but he didn't acknowledge me, either. Slowly, I pulled him to his feet, keeping him in a tight embrace. I was pretty sure the dead man was Wazi, and I had a good idea what had set Lucas off.

It had been a long time ago when we'd been in a Welsh pub one night after a long day of training with the British SAS. After more pints than I could remember, he'd told me how his little sister had been abducted, gang-raped and murdered. Her body had been found in a trash dumpster behind a meat packing plant.

He'd been deployed somewhere in southeast Asia at the time and hadn't found out about it until the police had already stopped investigating. They hadn't been able to find any suspects or witnesses to the crime. It had hit him especially hard because his parents had died in a car crash when he and his sister were young. A distant relative had taken them in, but Lucas had been the one who'd raised her.

As far as I knew, no one had ever been arrested for the crime. I'd never said anything to Lucas, but had always wondered if it had been targeted at him. It's not out of the realm of possibility for the bad guys we go after to try and retaliate. None of us are soft targets, but our families are a different story.

"What's wrong with him?" Hulk asked as I lead Lucas through the maze of rooms.

"Nothing," I said, shaking my head and giving him a look that sent a clear message to keep his mouth shut.

Nitro was waiting in the front room, giving me a questioning look when Lucas and I appeared.

"Spider?" I asked.

"In there." He nodded at the room where the women had been. "Found some clothes for the women."

"OK," I said, nodding. "Get Delker in there to document it."

He nodded and started to trot off to find the CIA agent.

"Nitro," I called.

He skidded to a stop and turned to look at me.

"I don't want Delker going anywhere else in this building. Just this room and the room where the women are. Understand me?"

He looked at me for a long moment, then shifted his eyes to Lucas before sliding them back.

"You got it, boss," he said, turned and dashed out the door.

I followed him out, still holding tight to Lucas. Turning to the side as soon as we exited the structure, I moved around the side of the building and leaned him against the chipped wall.

"Reaper five, area still clear?" I called on the radio.

"Affirmative," Poon answered immediately. "We moving?"

"Not yet," I said. "Sit tight and keep your eyes open."

"Copy that."

I should have been checking on the wounded and getting us moving. The sun would be coming up soon, and we had a long walk back to our camp. And, we had to do something with the women. We couldn't take them with us, but I wasn't about to leave them here.

"Reaper two, copy?" I called.

"Go," Spider said a moment later.

"Check our wounded and talk to our passenger for ideas about what to do with our new friends. Get the team ready to move in five minutes. Something I've gotta take care of."

"Copy," he said without hesitation.

Hunter's Rain

I turned to see Lucas looking at me. The madness had left his eyes, but they were vacant. I reached out and gently took each wrist, lifting them up between us. The rain was coming down steadily, washing the blood and mud from his raw fists.

"Keep 'em up," I said, releasing him and turning on my light for a better inspection.

"That was Wazi," he said in a low voice.

"I know," I said, gently probing each knuckle. "And you'll be glad to know you broke both your hands."

"Did I?"

He slowly looked down at them. Both were like swollen pieces of hamburger and several fingers were at angles that could only mean they were broken. The pain hadn't hit him yet, but when it did he was going to be one miserable son of a bitch.

"You kind of lost it," I said. "Gonna be able to get your shit together?"

There's a time and place to be sensitive to a friend's psychological trauma. The middle of a battlefield isn't one of them. There had been a lot of noise once the late Wazi's men had begun fighting back, and I had no idea who else might be within earshot. All I needed was another group of assholes to show up.

"I'm fine," he said after several seconds.

"Seriously, mate. We have to move, and I gotta know you've got your head in the game. We've got wounded, and we have to do something with the rest of those women."

He nodded and used a sleeve to wipe bloody rainwater off his face.

"I'm good to go," he said. "And… thanks."

I nodded.

"Just between us," I said. "I got the guys keeping Delker away. No sense in him getting any photos of that shit. Fucker doesn't need any leverage over you."

"I have to quit telling people you're an asshole," he said with a wan smile.

"Nah. Keep it up. Don't ruin my reputation."

22

Soon we were moving through the jungle. Lucas's hands were bandaged, and he was hurting like hell. Morphine would have helped, but it also would have made him unsteady on his feet. He and Mad Max were paired up near the center of the formation, a makeshift litter strapped to each of their shoulders. Two Step, unable to walk and goofy as hell on painkillers, lay strapped into the crude basket that swung between the two men. They might not have been in condition to fight, but by carrying the more seriously injured soldier, they freed up those of us who were.

We were on our way to a nearby village, which Delker knew of, to drop off the women. He was pissed at me for not having allowed him to wander around the building. I didn't care. He could make all the guesses he wanted about what had happened with Lucas, but I wasn't about to let him get photographic evidence. I'm not stupid enough to trust the CIA with anything that could be used against my friend.

It shouldn't be something any of us had to worry about, but it was. If Lucas had only shot Wazi in the head, he'd simply have been doing his job, and that would be the end of it. But, if evidence of how he'd beaten the man to death with his bare hands were to make it out to the media, or the right politician, he could wind up being charged with a war crime. Bullshit, I know, but that's how the fucked up world we live in works. So, I'd pissed Delker off and, if he wasn't already an enemy for life, he probably was now.

Most of an hour later, Hulk called a halt, and we went to ground. The sky to the east was steadily growing lighter, bathing the jungle in muted grays because of the dense cloud cover. It was still raining, and I was starting to wonder if it was ever going to stop or if we were in for another biblical cleansing. Not that this place couldn't use it.

The village was just ahead, and after a brief conversation we sent the women forward, alone. Delker had spoken with one of his assets who had assured him that the villagers would take them in and treat them well. That all sounded good, but I sent Poon to high ground with his rifle to keep an eye on how they were greeted. If there were any problems, I was prepared to go in and deal with them.

But, the man had been right. The refugees were welcomed, the village women descending on them and taking them in out of the rain. An old man, with grizzled white hair and a stooped back, stood in the rain after all of the women had disappeared. He leaned on a long staff, staring at the jungle in our direction. I still don't know why, but after nearly a minute I stood. Taking a few steps forward, I stopped when it was obvious he had seen me. I looked at him for a moment, then raised my arm and waved. After a beat, he nodded and hobbled away towards one of the larger huts.

We were quickly back on the trail, Hulk taking point as always. Mad Max and Lucas were both hurting like hell. I could see it in their faces, but neither complained and, despite the added weight of Two Step on the litter slung between them, they kept pace.

Two hours into our walk, the rain suddenly stopped. One second it was coming down in sheets, the next it was gone. Water continued to drip from the trees over our heads, but it was a physical relief to not have to move in a constant downpour. Twenty minutes later I wished for it to come back.

The clouds had broken, revealing an incredibly blue sky and brilliant sunshine. At first, this lightened everyone's mood, but that changed as the jungle began to heat up. The rain hadn't been cold, but it had kept the world around us cool. Now, as the sun beat down on the soupy mud, what had been pleasant humidity changed to stifling heat.

I've trained in the swamps of Georgia and Florida and the jungles of Panama. Operated in the tropical rain forests of Central America. I'm no virgin when it comes to heat, humidity and insects. But this was hell on earth.

Dirk Patton

As bad as the weather was, the bugs made it ten times worse. They rose from the jungle floor in clouds so thick I could hardly see ten feet. I had no idea what they were, and quickly learned that they were determined to crawl into my eyes, ears, nose... any exposed orifice. And, if they couldn't get in, the little fuckers started biting any bare skin.

Grumbling to myself, I wrapped a rain-soaked shemagh around my head and tied it tight before settling a pair of goggles in place. Once I was as protected as I could be, I called a brief halt and helped Lucas and Max cover up. Two Step was asleep from a dose of morphine, and when I leaned over him, I could see a swarm of the nasty little things dashing in and out of his nose and ears. Doing my best to clean them off, I wrapped his shemagh around his head, tucking it into his collar.

Armored as best we could, we kept moving. Steam was rising from the mud, adding to the misery and limiting our view into the surrounding jungle. Several times we heard gunfire, but it was distant and not in our direction of travel.

We stopped two more times, once to allow everyone to drink and adjust their clothing to better defend against the insects, then when we came to a fast running stream a mile short of our camp. It was no more than forty feet across, but the water was tumbling over round boulders as it rushed downhill. Yesterday, when we'd crossed it,

Hunter's Rain

there had only been a trickle meandering through the rocks near the center. Now, after a night of intense rain, it was brimming full.

This wouldn't normally have presented an issue. I'd send one of the team, usually Spider, to the far side by himself. He'd trail out a rope as he crossed, which would be secured to trees on either side. That would provide stability for the rest of the team as they walked on the slippery rocks in the swiftly running water. I would come last, bringing the line with me.

But we had wounded. One of them was on a litter and between the two litter bearers, there was only one good hand. We took a minute, getting burdens shifted, then Spider waded across with a rope tied around his waist. The water was really moving, and with the poor footing, he went down twice. He was swept several yards downstream before crawling out on the far bank.

Once the line was stretched taut and secured, Nitro stepped into the water. Two Step was slung across his bulging shoulders, tightly gripped with one hand. The other gripped the rope as he inched his way across the waist deep stream. While the rest of the team maintained watch on the surrounding jungle, I kept my eyes on my men, ready to plunge in if Nitro went down. But, he made it across without incident and gratefully handed Two Step off to Spider, who gently laid him face down on the ground.

One by one, I sent the rest of the team across. Hulk went with Lucas, a short length of rope tightly binding them together at the waist. Max made it on his own, offended when I asked if he needed someone to act as his anchor. The rest crossed with minimal problems, leaving me to untie the line and bring it with me.

The water was cold, and the current was strong as hell. I hadn't gone five feet into the stream when I slipped on a round rock and took a plunge. The rope pulled tight around my waist, arresting my tumble downstream and letting me get back to my feet. Hand over hand, I started walking up the line, falling four more times before I pulled myself onto the mud at Spider's feet.

"You are the whitest white man I've ever seen," he said, grinning and extending a hand to help me to my feet. "You got the coordination of a goddamn yak."

"That why I beat you at basketball every time?"

"That's because you play like it's a goddamn full contact sport. You ain't supposed to tackle the guy with the ball, dumbass."

Hunter's Rain

Before I could respond, there was the sound of gunfire from the direction of our camp. Several automatic rifles were firing, multiple bursts echoing down the mountain side. The team didn't need to be told what to do. Within seconds, all of us had melted into the surrounding jungle, leaving the narrow game trail we'd been following.

The firing continued for several seconds, then ceased as abruptly as it had begun. There was quiet for a moment, then a single weapon chattered out a long string of fire before falling silent.

23

We waited for several minutes but didn't hear any more gunfire. Hulk was out ahead of the group, and I quietly called him on the radio. He responded that everything was quiet at his position. Standing, I issued some brief orders to break the team up. Spider, Nitro, Hulk, Smyth and I were going to go forward and find out what the hell was going on. The rest would stay in place with our wounded until we called them forward.

It was a slow mile. We were moving with the utmost caution, and I let Hulk stay on point and set the pace. The jungle around us was coming back to life, all of the animals having gone quiet when the rifles had fired. Now, it was a constant cacophony of screeching birds and screaming monkeys.

Reaching the perimeter of our camp, we spread out in a long line, concealed in the bush. For several minutes we lay there, unmoving, as we scanned every inch of ground. Nothing had been disturbed, and there was no indication that there had been any uninvited guests poking around.

On my command, we all rose as one and stepped into the clear, rifles up and searching for threats. But there were none. Moving back into the shade of the trees, I looked at our surroundings, trying to figure out where the shooters had been. Glancing up at the sky, I paused when I saw two large birds slowly circling to our north. Up the slope of the mountain that loomed above us.

I caught each man's attention and hand signed where we were going. Hulk lead off a moment later, the rest of us spacing out into a single file line in his wake. He headed straight up the mountain, the trees thinning as we ascended. Frequently he would check the sky and adjust our direction based on the position of the vultures.

We climbed for half an hour, dropping to a knee when Hulk held up a clenched fist. I was second in line and could see him intently watching a small clearing to his front. A minute later, he waved for me to join him and I moved uphill to kneel by his side.

On the far side of the clearing were five bodies, partially hidden in tall grass. Other than what I assumed were corpses, and the birds overhead, nothing was moving. Not wanting to take the chance and reveal our presence too early, I split the team up. Nitro, Hulk and Smyth would circle around the clearing to our left while Spider and I went right.

Staying in the trees, we moved cautiously, pausing after every few steps to look and listen. Finally, we reached a spot that was closest to where the dead men lay. I signaled for everyone to stay in the cover of the jungle and took another long look around before stepping into the clearing.

My rifle was up, scanning the tree line as I moved. Closing to within twenty yards of the bodies, I shifted my focus to them and almost stopped in surprise. Only four of the dead were human. The fifth was a gorilla. What the fuck?

Weapon ready, I closed the final few yards and got my second surprise of the day. I'd expected the dead men to have been shot, but they'd been torn apart and beaten to death. At first blush, I thought they were the victims of a machete attack, but their wounds were nothing like what a sharp blade will inflict.

Arms were ripped free of bodies. Their heads were split open from immensely powerful blows. Rib cages had been crushed, collapsing in like tin cans. And blood was everywhere. Soaking their clothing and staining the dense carpet of grass that covered the clearing. And, the final surprise was that their skin wasn't black. At least what of it that was still visible.

Extending my foot, I hooked the toe of my boot under a shoulder and rolled the body over, frowning when I saw the face. Asian. Not Japanese or Thai. Most likely Korean or Chinese. Again… what the fuck?

Hunter's Rain

All of them were dressed in a camouflage pattern I didn't recognize as belonging to any specific country. Three of the four had AK rifles slung around their shattered bodies and pistols on their belts, but the fourth was completely unarmed. Kneeling, I took a closer look at the weapons, cursing under my breath when I saw that they were of Chinese manufacture.

The unarmed man lay closest to the gorilla. A large case was open, the contents strewn about, much of it crushed into the grass. Some of it I recognized, some of it I didn't. It all looked like things I'd seen in hospitals and doctor's offices.

Shifting around, I looked down at the dead gorilla. The animal was on its back, and there was an obvious bullet hole in its chest at the same point a human heart would be found. But that wasn't what commanded my attention. The scalp had been peeled back and the skull cut open, revealing its brain. A large syringe, with what I supposed was an equally large needle, was still inserted into the spongy tissue, sticking straight up.

"Reaper one, you need to see this."

Hulk's voice, suddenly coming over my radio earpiece, startled me. I turned toward the trees and spotted him when he waved. Moving quickly, I followed him into the jungle. I looked down when he pointed, spotting a blood trail.

Whoever it was couldn't have gone far. Not bleeding like that.

Within thirty yards, I began hearing labored breathing. At first, I thought he'd found a man who was still alive, but the sound wasn't right. When I stepped around a tree, I stopped in my tracks.

Ten feet away, leaned against a large rock, sat a mortally wounded gorilla. His massive arms were bloody to the elbows, and multiple bullet wounds to his chest and stomach were bleeding freely. He looked at me with a mixture of rage and pain in his eyes and tried to push himself to his feet, but collapsed back to the ground with a shudder.

I stood there, transfixed. Playing out in my head what must have happened. How he had fought the Chinese men who'd killed one of his family. The damage he'd inflicted, even as they fired their rifles into him at what must have been point blank range.

Looking up from his wounds, I met his eyes again. The rage was gone, replaced by the most profound sadness I've ever seen. How this animal could convey that emotion was beyond my ability to comprehend.

He coughed, bloody foam forming on his lips, then took a ragged breath and moaned. Maybe I was transferring too many human emotions onto the gorilla, but it felt as if he was mourning his loss, not expressing his physical pain. Slowly, without looking away from his gaze, I brought my rifle up and fired a single round into his head. Ending his suffering.

I stood there for another minute, just looking at him. There was no way to be certain, but I was convinced this was the same gorilla I'd come face to face with while pulling my watch. The one who'd simply been keeping an eye on his family to make sure I didn't try to harm them. Shaking my head, I turned and motioned for Hulk to lead the way back to the clearing.

While we walked through the jungle, I called the rest of the team on the radio and told them to come forward. I sent Hulk down the mountain to meet up with them at the camp. He would bring Doc and Delker back when they arrived. I had a sick feeling in the pit of my stomach that we'd just found the whole reason Doc had been sent along.

24

Doc had taken one look at the dead gorilla before digging through his pack and pulling out a whole stack of equipment. There were a couple of plastic tubes full of a cloudy liquid beneath one of the dead Chinese, and they went into sealed containers with bold biohazard labels on the outside. Then he'd set about taking some samples of his own.

While he worked, Delker had washed the dead men's faces clean of blood and taken several photos of each. When he was done with that, he severed the index finger from the right hand of each and put them in small tubes of some sort of preservative he carried in his pack.

"You just carry shit like that around with you?" Nitro asked.

He'd been watching the CIA agent closely as he worked. Delker ignored the question and searched the bodies, but found nothing other than gear for surviving in the jungle.

"Hey, boss. We may have a problem."

I'd been sitting at the edge of the tree line, watching Doc and Delker but not needing to be up close and personal with what they were doing. Poon's voice over the radio sent a jolt of adrenaline through me and I jumped up, looking to see the direction he was facing. Whipping around, I froze when I saw a group of gorillas at the upslope edge of the clearing. There were close to twenty, none nearly as large as the big male I'd put down earlier. Females and juveniles, I assumed. They stood together in a tight group, watching us.

"No one does anything if they don't attack," I called on the radio.

Truth is, it would have broken my heart if we'd had to kill any of them. But my men's lives were more important. I sincerely hoped they would just let us do what we needed to do and be on our way. Standing there, watching them, I wished I knew more about them.

"Doc. Delker," I said without turning my head. "Wrap it up. It's time to go."

"What the fuck are you talking about?"

The agent sounded as irritated as usual.

"You got two minutes," I said, not in any mood to debate the subject with him.

From the corner of my eye, I saw him start to straighten and look in my direction. Spider quickly stepped between us and hissed something that I couldn't hear. They stood looking at each other for a long moment before Delker began to gather his gear and pack it away.

"Doc, you good?" I asked, ignoring the exchange.

"Good as I'll be. I think I've got what I need," he said, also preparing to move.

It was a long, quiet walk down the hill to our camp. For some reason, even though it had been an act of mercy, shooting the gorilla had really affected me. Maybe I was just tired and had seen enough death for a while. All I wanted was to get the wet clothes and boots off and get some sleep.

Back in camp, we built a fire. Smyth had had the foresight to wrap a bunch of wood in a tarp so it didn't smoke too bad while burning. Otherwise, we'd have been sitting in a cold camp. Wet wood would have sent up a plume of smoke that could be seen for miles.

Holding my aching feet near the flames, I poured about a cup of water out of each boot before opening them up and putting them in the sun. Doc sat across from me, carefully examining the contents of the Chinese equipment case. The rest of the guys were drying out, or trying to, except for the two poor bastards that had pulled the first shift of sentry duty.

Hunter's Rain

Mad Max and Lucas were shot up with light doses of morphine and their injuries were given more treatment. I didn't see Delker at the moment but knew he'd wandered off into the trees to have a private conversation on his satellite phone.

"What the fuck were they doing, Doc?" I asked.

He looked up from the case of tools and hesitated. Finally, he shook his head.

"I'm sorry. I can't tell you."

I nodded, understanding as well as anyone that information is classified for a reason. And, if you start telling people things they have no legitimate need to know, pretty soon your secrets get out.

"But," he said, lowering his head to examine a particularly wicked looking instrument. "If they're doing what I think they're doing, this is some really scary stuff."

I sat there looking at him. Not saying anything. I knew if I asked, he'd clam up. But, he obviously wanted to talk, and I wasn't going to stop him if he did.

"Rabies," he finally said.

"What?" I asked, surprised.

"They're after samples of simian rabies," he said, still not looking up.

"Why? And why here?"

"*Here* is the largest wild population of great apes on the planet," he said. "And they also carry what's called Silent Rabies. It doesn't show and doesn't do to them what you think of when you hear rabies. They don't become Cujo. But, in a few documented cases from gorilla researchers, something has activated the virus and, when that happens, they go on a nearly unstoppable rampage. They're far stronger and more dangerous than an ape infected with…"

I wanted to hear more, but Nitro chose that moment to walk up with his laptop in hand.

"Gotta call in, boss," he said.

With a groan, I stood and rummaged through my gear until I found my sat phone. Stepping away, I powered it up, waited for it to lock onto an orbiting bird and initiated a call to JSOC (Joint Special Operations Command). The conversation was brief, as they always are. Powering down the handset, I tossed it in my pack.

"Nitro, pass the word," I said, picking up my wet boots. "They're pulling us out. Aussies, too."

Hunter's Rain

"Seriously?" Spider looked up from an MRE that he was busily inhaling. "What the fuck? There's still more of these assholes that need a late night visit."

"UN is finally getting involved," I said. "JSOC wants us out of here before any of them start showing up. The White House and Canberra are worried about it getting out that they had troops in-country."

"Fucking pussies," Spider mumbled.

I had to agree with him. Not that I wouldn't be happy to get the hell out of this nightmare, but these people needed help. The kind of help we were giving them. The kind of help the UN wouldn't.

"We're pulling out," Delker said, coming out of the jungle behind me.

"Yep. Just got the word," I said.

"Yeah, well, you'll get some more words when you get home. I just talked to my boss about how you kept me out of that mission and then hurried me here. Didn't let me do my job. You were supposed to cooperate, not fuck things up. He's going to call your Colonel and have a little chat about what cooperation really means."

I had turned to look at him as he spoke, staring at the smug expression on his face.

"Fuck you, Delker," I said tiredly. "Just fuck you. I don't even care."

"You will," he said, almost gloating. "You see, that pretty little wife of yours is CIA, too. We'll see how her career…"

He stopped talking and stared at me with his mouth open when I drew my pistol and pointed it at his face. Time stretched out as I fought the urge to move my finger off the frame of the weapon and pull the trigger.

"You'll never get away with it," he breathed after a long beat.

I was aware that Spider and Nitro were standing behind me. Silent. Waiting. I knew that if I pulled the trigger, they'd back up whatever story I decided to spin that would explain how Delker had died in Africa. But, I didn't want to put them in that position, even though I'd do the same for them without thinking twice.

Lowering the gun, I clicked the safety back on and thrust it into its holster. Looking around, I saw that Doc was intently staring at the Chinese tools, obviously ignoring what was transpiring.

Hunter's Rain

"You say whatever you want about me," I said, staring hard at Delker. "I'll deal with any shit that comes my way. But. You fuck with my wife. Even breathe her name to anyone. I'll find you. You need to forget all about her. You, and your limp dick brother. Because, if you cause her any problems. Even one. If she gets demoted, transferred, boxed out, or even a hangnail, I'll blame you. You wanna come for me? Take your best shot. Go after her, I will end your fucking life. Do we understand each other?"

He stared back at me for a long time, looking into my eyes as he tried to judge if I was serious. Finally, he blinked and looked away. Turned and walked to the far side of camp, ignoring me. And, that was just fine.

"Sorry about that, Doc," I said when I'd cooled down a bit.

"About what?" He asked, looking up for the first time and smiling.

Epilogue

Seventy-two hours later I walked down the ramp of a C-130 that had just landed at Pope Air Force Base in North Carolina. It had been an excruciatingly long flight, especially in an aircraft as noisy and uncomfortable as the Hercules. But, we were home.

A truck was waiting to take us to the clubhouse on Fort Bragg, and we all piled in. Two Step had been evac'd on an Air Force C-40 that had taken him to Ramstein Air Base in Germany. It didn't make sense to me that he'd been taken there rather than brought back to the states, but that's the way the military works. No point in trying to figure it out.

Doc had taken the same flight with his samples, and Delker had disappeared as soon as we'd reached Australia. Lucas and Mad Max were whisked away to be seen by specialists, and the rest of us had slept until our ride arrived. Then we'd slept for much of the flight home. Now, all I wanted was to dump my gear and go see Katie, but that wouldn't happen as fast as I'd like.

There'd be a couple of humorless guys from Army Intelligence waiting to see the team and me. I'm not one to pull rank, but this time, I fully intended to. They were going to debrief me first so I could get the hell out of there.

It was late morning, though my body had no idea what day or time it should be. When we pulled up at the barracks, I wasn't surprised to see two Army staff cars sitting in the parking area. Climbing down, I lead the way inside, the guys already grumbling about having to talk to the stiff dicks from intel. But, we got it over with, and surprisingly, they didn't ask very many questions.

In less than half an hour, the intelligence officer, a Chief Warrant Officer, thanked me for my time and slapped his notebook closed. He'd taken all of three lines of notes.

"That's it?" I asked in surprise.

Nothing in the Army ever happens this fast. I'd been expecting hours of debriefing, at a minimum. But then, sometimes there are things that the brass really doesn't want to know too much about. He nodded and got up, heading for the door. Reaching for the knob, he paused and looked back at me.

"Off the record," he said.

"Oooohhh K," I answered, not liking where this was going.

"Did you really threaten to kill the CIA agent that was with you? Delker?"

I looked at him for a long beat, not sure where he might have heard that little nugget.

"I'm sure he misunderstood me," I said, not about to admit anything, on or off the record. "Things were a little hectic."

He stood there with his hand on the knob, looking at me.

"Watch your ass," he finally said. "From what I hear, he's a vindictive son of a bitch."

He'd turned and left without anything further. I sat there for a bit, then dismissed the whole thing from my mind and headed for the shower. When I came out, Spider was waiting for me with a shit eating grin on his face.

"What?"

"You must be doing something right," he said, smirking. "But I don't know how. Guess she's got low standards or something."

"What the fuck are you talking about?"

"Main gate called. Seems there's this pretty little red headed girl with a CIA badge waiting for you. Hmmm. Pretty little red headed girl. Makes me think of Peanuts."

Hunter's Rain

"You're making less sense than usual," I said, mood already lightened at the prospect of seeing Katie.

I shouldn't have been surprised that she was able to find out when I was arriving. Not with her job.

"Peanuts, dumbass," Spider said as we headed for the parking lot. "You know. Charlie Brown? Snoopy? You even kinda look like Charlie Brown with your head shaved! Now all you need is a dog!"

"Shut the fuck up and give me a ride to the gate, Pigpen."

Printed in Great Britain
by Amazon